Maple

Creek

By

Elizabeth Penn

*This book is dedicated to David Simmons,
with special thanks to Jack Barr.*

Chapter 1

My mouse hovered over the options under "Status" for my social profile. The cursor glided between "Separated" and "It's Complicated." Which one was correct?

I mean, technically, we were going to be separated. He was here in California, and I would soon be in New England. But there was no official paperwork filed. I was just going to go. But if I said it was complicated, well, that wasn't exactly true either. There was nothing complicated about it. He hit me, and I packed my bags. Although, it wasn't the first time he had hit me, and I don't know why it took me as long as it did to leave. Maybe it *was* complicated.

I clicked the 'x' button, closing out of the window, leaving my status as "Married" until I could make up my mind. Then, closing my laptop and slipping it into my purple suitcase along with the charger, I walked out the front door into the early morning air to catch my taxi to the airport. Hector had gone to work early, and he wasn't expecting to see me for at least a few hours.

My purse was full of wads of cash that I had saved up for over a year. And with it, I bought my plane ticket. I can't really explain what the plane ride felt like. I wasn't crying and devastated over my decision. But I wasn't joyous and happy either. I was numb. The whole situation didn't feel good or bad. It simply was.

After a seemingly never-ending day of flights, my final plane landed in the small-town airport of Maple Creek, my hometown. I'd been away almost 10 years. With my luggage click-clacking behind me, I walked out into the crisp night air. I'd forgotten a jacket since I wasn't used to the cold weather, and goosebumps ran up my arms the moment the automatic doors whooshed open.

I reached into my pocket for my phone so I could order an Uber. I didn't know exactly how long I would be gone or if my money would stretch far enough for me to rent a car for my entire trip. But my phone wasn't in my pocket. I'd forgotten that I'd left it behind. Phones could be tracked.

So, instead, I made my way down the empty sidewalk to the pick-up area, which was illuminated with yellow streetlights. I paid for a ride from the airport shuttle to take me from the airport to the local Bed and Breakfast. I couldn't help but look back over my shoulder as I climbed into the van. The driver shut the sliding door behind me, and it locked with a click.

Due to the late season, the sun had already almost completely set, and in turn, the buildings were now nothing but glowing white windows between the trees. That was, aside from the square and the few houses around town, which were completely decked out in Halloween decorations. Their yards were scattered with jack-o-lanterns and plastic cemeteries, which were lit up with flashing strobe lights.

The B&B, too, was decorated for the season. Pumpkins and squash lined the walkway, and paper ghosts hung in the trees. I hadn't celebrated the holiday since I was little, and the decorations made me feel like a child again. Only, there was no one to hold my hand this time, and I was alone to face the ghosts in town.

I walked up the short flight of steps to the door. The house was all red brick with white shutters and a dark blue door, much like the traditional American home you would see featured on postcards or in oil paintings. The door opened to a simple foyer with wooden floors, which, while a bit worn, were still beautiful. There was a matching wood table, which held a smiling jack-o-lantern, and above it hung a small Tiffany chandelier.

On the left of the foyer was an empty dining room with another door on the far wall which read 'kitchen.' And on the right was another open door which led to a cozy-looking living room with a roaring fire in a small brick fireplace. In the back of the foyer, on the other side of the table, sat an antique grandfather clock beside a wide wooden staircase which led to the second floor. The air smelled strongly of pumpkin spice.

Out of the kitchen swooped in a tiny elderly woman with silver hair done up in a messy bun.

"Oh, hello! You must be Emily Heart," she said cheerfully, wiping her hands off on her sunflower apron.

"Yes, I am."

"Perfect! My name is Margaret Davies. I'm just getting dinner ready. Your room is up the stairs, the last door on the left. The Pink Room. You'll love it!" she squeaked.

"Thank you. Is the dinner for everyone, or…"

3

"Yes. Well, for everyone that is here. We have breakfast every morning and dinner on most nights. It's just you right now, but in a few weeks, when the holidays come around, we get kind of crowded."

"If you call a small handful of people crowded," chuckled a man who entered the room from the kitchen, "We only have three rooms to rent here, Grams."

"Oh, this is John Wood," the woman explained, "My grandson. He helps me run the place. You must try his pumpkin pies. He just pulled them out to cool."

"Sounds yummy," I smiled, "I mean, the pie sounds yummy, not John. I mean, not that you aren't. I just meant…"

"And you are?" he asked, interrupting my rant and offering his hand.

"Emily," I answered, taking it.

"It's nice to meet you, Emily."

John was tall and slim. He had hazel eyes which were framed by thick black-framed glasses, and his hair was in messy brown locks. He wore a cream sweater over a pair of tight tattered jeans. He was barefoot.

"John, help her with her suitcase. I have to get back to cooking," Margaret said, scurrying back through the dining room.

"You don't have to," I said, reaching for the handle on my bags. But he was faster, and he was already carrying it up the first few steps before I could reach it.

"I know I don't have to. But I want to."

"Well, thank you," I blushed. I wasn't used to a kind hand.

I loved The Pink Room, just as Margaret had said that I would. It was quaint and simple, like a bedroom you would find in a cottage. The wallpaper was a soft rose color, and there was a light wood vanity dresser with a single paper rose in a small crystal vase by the mirror. The bed was covered in a pink rose quilt with frilly lace pillows.

John set my suitcase beside the vanity, and I crossed the room to look out the window. The view looked over the backyard, which had two large barren trees and a patio decorated with strings of lights and a few metal tables and chairs.

"You know, bringing girls to my room isn't usually my first move, I promise," he laughed.

"What?"

"This used to be my room before everything was remodeled. I grew up here. Sorry, it was just a joke," he said, his face flushing a bit as he shoved his hands into his pockets.

I looked back out the window.

"So," he continued, "Your hair is cut pretty short for cold weather. Where are you from?"

I'm from here, I thought. But I needed a fresh start, not to drudge up old memories. I was already lucky that John hadn't recognized me from school or some other place in the small town.

"California," I answered.

"Very cool. Well, I should get back down to help finish dinner. It should be ready in about half an hour or so. See you there?"

"Yeah. Sounds good. Thanks for helping me with my bags."

He gave me a wink, closing the door behind him. I sat down on the edge of the bed, falling back onto the mattress. It was soft, and I sank down into it. I lay there for a few minutes, listening to the silence. The gravity of what I had done finally hit me. I was alone in Maple Creek. I was free.

Chapter 2

I made my way downstairs to the dining room, following the sweet smell of spices. The stairs creaked beneath my feet, and the banister was a bit loose, but the aged house was made homey by the lace curtains and oil paintings that hung on the walls.

The table was lit up by orange candles which were surrounded by blue and white ceramic plates that were covered in mountains of food. Potatoes, three-bean salads, and some sort of baked fish left barely any room for dining, but it looked delicious.

I took a seat across from John, who was in the middle of a tense conversation with his grandmother. He was leaning back in his chair, fidgeting with his fork, while his grandmother lunged across the table at him, begging.

"Please, John? We need to be more active in the community and get some advertising out there," she pleaded.

"I'm not going if you aren't," he shrugged.

"You know I can't do these sorts of things. I'm an old woman, John. I'm fragile."

"Well, I'm not going alone."

They already had some untouched food on their plates, so I quietly spooned a glob of mashed potatoes onto my own, hoping not to draw too much attention and get pulled into the conversation.

"Emily could go with you," Margaret smiled, sitting back down and taking a bite of fish.

I froze, looking back and forth between them.

"No, Grams. I don't think Emily should be pulled into doing a PR stunt on her vacation," John said, shaking his head.

"She's booked until February! She has all the time in the world to go sightseeing later. And besides, since she is staying here, she can talk up the place. This is a great way for her to meet the people in town."

"May I ask, exactly what are we talking about?" I interjected.

Margaret leaned over, squeezing my hand, "There is a fabulous little adult-only Halloween party at the Town Hall tomorrow night. The whole town will be there. I told John he should represent the B&B."

Part of me didn't want to go so I could avoid running into people I might know. But I was also curious to see how things had changed.

"I don't have a costume," I answered, thinking that might be the end of it.

"They should have a few left in the stores downtown," Margaret said, "What do you say?"

I glanced across the table at John, who flashed a crooked smile at me.

"I'll go if John is going."

"Perfect!" exclaimed Margaret, "John, you're going."

I placed some fish on my plate, hiding my smile behind a napkin. John's relationship with his grandmother was amusing.

"So, what brings you to Maple Creek, Emily?" John asked.

"I'm taking some time for myself to find my passions again. I'm hoping to look around and maybe get settled into a place here if it goes well."

"Isn't that kind of the purpose of California?" he asked.

"I have too many ties there. And my life wasn't exactly the glamorous California dream."

"What did you do there?" Margaret asked.

"I was a secretary at Jacobson's Enterprises. Just one of those paperwork and staplers sort of jobs."

"I've heard of Jacobson's," John said, taking a sip of wine.

"Must have been a nice paycheck at such a fancy corporation," his grandmother added.

"I suppose," I muttered, focusing again on my dinner.

My bank account would read $200 every other Friday: my allowance from my husband. The rest of my money was a direct deposit into his account. He had updated my paperwork to reflect what he had told me was a joint bank account back when we were dating. He said it was a gift, as a symbol of taking our relationship more seriously. It was definitely serious.

I was dating Hector Jacobson, one of the heirs to the Jacobson fortune. He was working for his father until it was his turn to take over the company. He was handsome and attentive, powerful, controlling, and eventually abusive. But not until I had a ring on my finger.

The rest of the dinner was quiet as we all finished our fish. After the necessary pleasantries, I slipped away back up the stairs to my room. I laid my clothes aside, crawled under the covers, and drifted off to sleep. I didn't have any dreams.

Chapter 3

The next morning I woke around seven, and I could already hear the clanging of pots and pans downstairs in the kitchen. I picked out a cool-weather outfit to include a red sweater, skinny jeans, and a pair of black heels. Heels were the only type of shoes I had anymore, because they were all that Hector said looked nice on me. I took the outfit with me, down to the bathroom at the end of the hallway for a morning shower.

While parts of the house had been modernized, the bathroom definitely had not. The shower was not a shower, but instead, was a claw-foot bathtub, which had been pushed under a rusty faucet coming from the wall. The toilet, which was much smaller and closer to the ground than I was used to, flushed with the pull of a wooden handle attached to a yellow-gold chain. There were no real decorations, with the exception of a tray of decorative soaps on the sink.

I turned two squeaky handles on the bathtub faucet, and the water switched between boiling hot and freezing cold no matter how carefully I turned the knobs. After a few minutes of trying to get it right, I settled on lukewarm and climbed into the tub.

The gentle splash of the water reminded me a bit of those Zen gardens that dripped water onto rocks at dentist offices or those kinds of houses that hosted dinner parties. But just like in those venues, there was still a tightness in my chest. A weight that had me gripping the edges of the tub, trying not to be pulled under the water. I could feel a panic attack trying to take over my thoughts, so I tried to focus on the bath.

I reached over onto the sink, plucking a seashell soap from the pile in the tray. It smelled of old perfume and garden herbs. Upon touching the water, it melted, turning the bathwater into milk.

My fingertips rippled the surface as the white creamy liquid danced on my skin, washing me clean. I ran my hands down my legs, up across my stomach and chest, and back down my arms. I winced as the milky white liquid washed over the bluish-gray lines on my upper right arm, almost perfectly outlining a handprint. It had been hidden beneath the sleeve of my shirt the day before, and I had almost completely forgotten about it.

I took a pause, letting the water continue dripping down my skin. Then, I took a handful of the water and splashed it over my face, removing the thick-coated makeup to reveal the matching bruise on my left cheek. A tear fell down my cheek, mixing with the water.

With a deep breath, I dunked back into the water, allowing my body to relax in the sloshing silence as the liquid soap enveloped me, dissolving the dirt of the past, and I sat up again, meditating in the silence. After a few more minutes, I stepped out of the tub, pulling the plug, and wrapping a scratchy off-white towel around myself and dabbing the drops of moisture from my legs.

Once I had put on my clothes, I dried off my hair with the towel, causing it to stick out every which way like yellow hay, as Hector used to say. I looked up in the mirror as I patted down my hair.
My face looked much worse than I had imagined. The extra day had set the colors of the bruise deeper into my skin. Without makeup to cover it up again, I had to try and make it back to the room without being spotted. Just as luck would have had it, as that thought crossed my mind, there was a knock on the door beside me.

"I'm in here! Sorry. Almost done. I'll be out in a minute," I shouted, probably a little louder than necessary.

"No problem, don't be sorry," I heard the voice of John say from the other side of the door, "I just always make sure to knock. You know, since there is no lock on the door."

I looked down to see if he was right. There was no lock on the door. I covered my face with my hand, looking around for a way to get out of the room without having to answer any questions. I spotted my towel and snatched it back off the rack, pretending to dry my hair again as I opened the door, pushing past John.

"All yours," I said casually.

Before I could make it two steps past him, I felt the door click shut behind me, and the towel was ripped from my head, uncovering my face. I looked back to see the corner of the towel was caught in the door, and John's eyes were wide open.

13

"Oh, my goodness. Are you alright?" he asked, obviously concerned.

"Um, yes. Of course. I just…" I stuttered.

"Fell in the tub?"

I nodded silently. I was never very good at lying.

"I'll get some slip grips for the bathtub later today. Bathtubs can be dangerous."

"Thank you," I muttered, turning to go back to my room.

John caught my hand, "Emily? I'm here if you need someone to talk to. I know how it is. My mother used to fall all the time, too."

My heart sank as I looked back at him. His eyes were soft behind his wide-rimmed glasses, and his lips smiled in a sad sort of way. Then, squeezing my hand, he went into the bathroom, and I went back to my room to hide my bruises again.

Chapter 4

Eggs, toast, and sausage were all out on the table by the time I went downstairs.

"Good morning, Miss Emily. Coffee?" asked Margaret.

"Yes, please."

"Cream? Sugar?"

"Just cream, thank you."

"Any ideas for your costume tonight?" she asked excitedly, setting the mug down in front of me.

"No. It's been years since I wore a costume. I'm just going to see what they have left."

"Well, there is a grocery store down the street. It doubles as a general store, too. It's called…"

"Maple Market," I interjected. It just sort of slipped out.

"Yes," she smiled, "Nice to see you still remember some of this place."

"Wait, what?"

"Good morning, lovely ladies," John said, entering the room.

"Coffee, John?" Margaret asked.

"I'll have mine in a to-go mug this morning, Grams. I have to run into town and pick up a few things," he answered.

"You and Emily should go together."

"Grams," he sighed, "First of all, Emily probably doesn't like always being talked about like she isn't here. And second, I'm going to the hardware store, not the grocery. I have to pick up some supplies to reattach the light fixture in your bedroom, and I need to get some slip grips for the bathtub."

"Slip grips?" Margaret asked with a raised eyebrow.

"Yeah, I noticed how slippery it was this morning, and I wanted to be sure to fix it before the rest of the guests arrive in a few weeks," he explained.

"Okay, darling. Whatever you think we need," Margaret shrugged, pouring John some coffee.

The coffee was sweet and hot. It was served in a white mug with a faded symbol on the side, like the ones you would get as a souvenir from a road trip. I was trying to make out the letters on the mug when John took a seat beside me.

"However," he said with a smile, putting his extra-large to-go mug on the table beside mine, "If you would like a ride into town, I would be more than happy to take you."

"I'd like that. I didn't end up renting a car," I answered, "Just let me finish my coffee, and I'll be ready to go."

"Neither of you have even touched your breakfast yet," Margaret squeaked, throwing her hands up.

"Take your time," he winked at me, grabbing a piece of sausage and taking a bite. He put his arm around Margaret and kissed her head, "Thanks, Grams. Breakfast looks great."

I placed an egg on a piece of toast, cutting it open so that the bright yellow liquid soaked the bread and flooded my plate. John had taken his seat beside me again, nibbling at some sausages. To be honest, I usually didn't mind being invisible. But John made it nice to be noticed. Not watched. Just noticed.

His car was a beat-up silver something or other. I was never very good at identifying cars. It was small but functional. The inside was soft black fabric, and it smelled like cotton. The backseat was covered in tools, ropes, and electrical cords, which I assumed were from some of his unfinished projects.

He didn't look much like a handyman, though. If anything, he reminded me a little bit of a hipster. He didn't come across as the powerful, intimidating type that I was used to, but he was still strong. His plaid shirt was loose and untucked, and yet, he still looked refined in his own sort of way.

I'd recognized his last name when we were introduced. I figured we might have had a class together in elementary school, or maybe I saw him in the halls of the high school before I moved away. But I didn't really know him.

The images that passed outside the window of bright orange trees, brick buildings, and joggers who were all wrapped up in hats and scarves all looked like a dream to me. Although not my own dream. I had never dreamed of going back to Maple Creek. The town had nothing left for me. Not after my parents died, which was shortly after my leaving. I'd dropped out of school, moved out West, and never looked back.

I felt John's hand on my leg, giving it a squeeze and making me jump, "Emily? We're here."

The car had come to a stop, and we were pulled up to the storefront of the Maple Market. I had no idea how long we had been there. I hadn't even noticed we'd stopped.

"I'll be just down the street at the hardware store, but I'll be quick. I'll swing back as soon as I'm done."

"Okay. Thanks for the ride," I said, giving him a smile and stepping out of the car.

"And, Emily?"

"Yes?"

"You're going to be okay."

My hand came up involuntarily to the bruise on my face. I tried to play it cool and continued through with the motion, brushing my hair behind my ear.

"Of course I will. I'm just picking out a costume," I smiled.

He nodded slowly, and I shut the door, practically running into the store.

Chapter 5

My chest was tight, and my ears rang as I made my way up and down the maple market aisles. It was terrifying, which I hadn't expected. The store was just as I had remembered it. There were a few updates, such as the new cash registers and a fresh coat of paint, but the rest was exactly like it was in my memories.

The floors were blue and white checkered, and the shelves in the aisles were just short enough that you could see over the tops to the next aisle without straining too much. All of the items were off-brand or local goods, and most of the price tags were unbelievably low compared to what I had gotten used to in California.

On the right side of the store was all the food, and on the left were the home goods, clothes, and a small pharmacy. In the back of the clothes aisle was a seasonal section, which that day was stocked with plastic turkeys, cornucopias, and a few Christmas wreaths and trees that were already starting to take over the aisle.

In the far back corner, I could see a plastic skeleton with a missing arm peeking around at me from behind one of the trees. On a hook, just above him, was an assortment of leftover costumes. There was an adult, extra-large, male grim reaper, a girl's size small princess, two teenage cowboy costumes, and the squished way in the back was the only woman's costume left: a black cat.

It wasn't even a good cat costume. The plastic bag on the hook contained a pair of cardboard ears on a headband, a clip-on tail that looked like it was made from a feather boa, a pair of fluffy gloves, and a little makeup set of black and pink gel goo.

I looked at the sticker on the bag and cringed. They wanted $30 for that sad getup. I shook my head at the thought of showing up to the party like that. *This must be what a High School Reunion feels like*; I thought to myself as I took the bag to the register.

"Just now getting your costume?" the teenage cashier teased, putting the costume in a small white bag. She tapped her fingers on the touch screen, her black and orange manicure clicking against it as she did. "That'll be $31.65."

"Thanks," I mumbled, taking out a wad of cash from my pocket and handing her forty.

"Haven't seen you around. Are you new here?" she asked, making my change.

"I'm visiting."

"Well, it's pretty nice here. There is a Halloween party in town tonight. My parents go every year, and they love it. And if you are ever looking for anything fun to do locally, there is a corkboard up near the front doors where people can post events, classes, and yard sales. $8.35 is your change. Have a happy Halloween."

I took the change, put it back in my pocket, and scooped up my plastic bag. I couldn't see John's car in the parking lot yet, so I took her suggestion and wandered over to the corkboard. A flier was posted for a children's book reading at the local library on Saturday mornings. I used to go to it when I was little, and I was happy to see it was still there.

There were also papers posted for holiday events at local restaurants, a few homemade signs made with Sharpies for yard sales, and a 'lost dog' flier with a picture of some sort of scraggly chihuahua.

I heard the crackle of pavement as John's car rolled up outside the automatic doors. But just before I walked away from the board, a colorful stock image of a paintbrush caught my eye. I lifted up one of the yard sale fliers to see that underneath was an advertisement for painting classes.

Adult Painting Classes
Tuesday Nights @ 6
In the Gym at
Maple Creek Elementary
$5

A smile spread across my face. I used to love painting. In fact, I did it almost every day until I started working at Jacobson's. By the time Hector and I were married, my art supplies had been so far from my mind that they somehow ended up in the trash pile during a spring cleaning of our house. I looked over the flier one more time, making a mental note of the place and time before passing through the doors and taking my seat in the passenger seat of John's car.

"Hey. Were you able to find a costume?" he asked, shifting the car into gear and pulling out of the parking lot.

"I guess you could call it a costume," I shrugged.

"Yeah, they seem to skip from holiday to holiday pretty fast around here. I'm glad you were able to find something, though."

"How was the hardware store?"

"It was good. They had everything I needed," he said, pointing to the bag in the back, "I'm going to make sure no bathtubs hurt you again. Not while I'm around."

A warmth spread through my chest, and my shoulders relaxed a bit. His voice was sincere. He made my face hurt, too. But not from the bruise. Instead, it hurt from the smile I couldn't seem to control the whole ride back to the B&B.

Chapter 6

The costume was an even bigger disaster out of the bag. The ears sat crooked on my head, and the face paint looked like I had a bright pink highlighter on my nose. I decided to put on my black sweater for the party to try and make my clothes match the costume a bit. At least it was slimming.

It was just past four o'clock when the first trick-or-treaters started to arrive. John was answering the door, passing out handfuls of lollipops and mini chocolate bars from a large plastic bin that was shaped like a cauldron. Meanwhile, Margaret was in the kitchen cooking an early dinner for us. I snuck out the back door quietly on my way to visit my own Halloween ghosts.

The backyard was cozy. The metal tables and chairs gave it a café-style feeling, and the late afternoon sun set the autumn leaves ablaze in the tall maples. There was no fence, so I was able to slip down the street silently and into the surrounding neighborhood.

The trees seemed to get larger as I walked, and their shadows grew darker. I wandered the sidewalks until the scenery felt familiar again, and I could feel the pull of old memories leading me down the lane. I could hear the heavy bells chiming in the steeple of the old

Catholic church as I rounded the corner to my destination.

The graveyard appeared through the trees, enclosed by a spiked metal gate. Across the street from the church, tucked into a mess of overgrown shrubs, was a small cottage with chipped white siding and a red door; my childhood home.

I opened the cold metal gate to the cemetery and entered, taking my time as I stepped carefully around the gravestones. My heart was heavy, and my feet dragged through the dry grass. My steps crunched beneath me to the other side of the graveyard.

Many of the gravestones were old and worn, some of which were completely faded and unreadable with moss and cracks all over their faces. I stopped beside a set of shiny newer gravestones which sat snuggly against the back wall of the church, and I read the names out loud: Robert Heart and Mary Heart. My parents. Their death dates were only one day apart.

They had been strict, running a house of discipline, repentance, and piousness. We attended mass every week together as a family and went to church a second time each week to attend confession. Even when I was very little, I was kept pristine. My clothes were plain and humble, and I was always looking down at my shiny black shoes. Not a word came from my lips. Children were to be seen, not heard.

When I turned 16, I cut off my long golden locks and ran away to the West Coast with a group of friends. We fell out shortly after, but I was able to find a job as a low-level secretary at a dental office. That was where I met Hector Jacobson. We started dating, and shortly after he filled out paperwork hiring me at his company as his personal secretary.

That Christmas, I had opted out of seeing my parents when they invited me back home. I left with the intention of never going back, and I meant to keep it that way. But that same week, their car, like many others that year, had spun out on the ice and tumbled into a ditch. My father died in the car, and my mother died in the hospital the very next day. Hector didn't give me the time off to go to the funeral. And part of me, at the time, didn't want to go.

I knelt down by the stones, tracing the names with my frozen fingertips. Halloween was the day that the dead were said to walk the Earth, but the graveyard was empty and silent. The wind picked up, rustling the dead leaves around me. They weren't there. They were gone. I had begun to shiver. I had forgotten how frigid the air was as the sun set in Maple Creek.

I picked a few stray leaves from the headstones, and with a single tear, I turned and left, going back to the B&B. The walk back was freezing as the sun sank down, but I was still too uneasy to go inside the house. I slumped down into one of the deck chairs out back, laying my head down on the cold metal table. I felt dizzy, and I tried to focus on my breathing as my breath hung in an icy cloud in front of me.

Behind me, I heard John's heavy steps come up behind me and stop. I didn't move.

"You okay?" he asked, placing a hand on my shoulder.

I sighed, sitting up and re-adjusting my flimsy cat ears, "Yeah, I'll be okay."

"Do you want to talk about it?"

I shook my head.

"Well, dinner is ready. And if there is anything in this world that can cheer me up when I'm down, it's stuffing my face with pumpkin pie."

I cracked a smile, "Can't argue with that."

"Good! Here, let me help you up. You make a cute cat, by the way."

"Thanks. Are you putting on your costume after dinner?"

"Yeah, mine is a bit hard to eat in."

I followed him into the warm house and almost immediately the feeling began to come back into my face. Dinner was a delicious herb roasted chicken with corn on the cob and pumpkin pie. John poured Margaret and I each a mug of hot apple cider from a pot on the stove, which I assumed he spiced himself. And, to finish off the holiday spread, he placed an orange bowl in the center of the table that was overflowing with candy.

Everything on the table had that homemade feel to it, and I found it comforting, which was probably why I ate more than I should have. The conversations were light and Margaret didn't have time to get pushy about anything in particular because the doorbell was ringing constantly with eager children giggling and grasping for candy.

Stuffed, I returned my plate to the sink and took a minute to go to the bathroom and touch up my makeup while John was putting on his costume for the party. When I was finished, I waited for him in the living room on the light blue velvet couch. The walls

26

were painted cream and were decorated with old family photos. A few of which I could see were of Ms. Margaret when she was much younger and a baby I assumed was John.

On the opposite side of the couch was a white fireplace covered in Halloween decorations, including fake spider webs, bleeding candles, and a plastic jack-o-lantern. I could hear John's steps approaching and turned to see him enter the room with a black and red cape fluttering behind him. His face was painted white, and his hair was slicked back.

"Lewts duh dis," he garbled, smiling at me through a pair of plastic white vampire teeth.

I couldn't help but laugh, and I started to feel a little better about my own costume. We walked out to his car, and he opened the car door for me. Everything felt so normal, but my stomach still hurt.

Chapter 7

I was glad I was wearing black. I could already feel sweat stains forming on my sweater as we entered through the main doors of the town hall. My hair was shorter, and my face was more mature than the last time I had been to the town. I was also dressed like a cat, and I was hoping that would be enough to not be recognized.

The conference room that they had transformed into a room for the Halloween party actually looked pretty great. There were streamers of black, silver, and orange hanging from the ceiling. The snack table was cleverly skeleton-themed with a punch bowl in the shape of a skull, and the finger foods were all stacked up in plastic ribcages. Over the speakers, they played holiday classics like the 'Monster Mash' while a small group of people danced in the strobe lights.

"Shall I get us some drinks?" John asked, spitting through his fangs.

The thought of him leaving my side at the party made me uncomfortable. I didn't want to hang out on the side like a wallflower, all awkward like a school dance, and even worse, I didn't want to be recognized and pulled into a conversation by someone I wasn't exactly excited to see.

"No, that's okay. I'll get the drinks. You are supposed to be here to mingle. I'll find you," I answered.

"Okay, Miss Independent," he smiled.

I hugged the wall, making my way around to the punchbowl and spooning the blood-red juice into two clear plastic cups. My eyes scanned the room for John, who had already joined in with the crowd. I found him in the middle of the floor, laughing and swaying to the music with a small circle of people.

I carefully made my way through the crowd to reach him, brushing up against a few people as I passed and doing my best to protect my face paint from rubbing off on anyone or, even worse, spilling the drinks on them. I handed John his drink, and the laughing died down as he introduced me to his friends.

"Everyone, this is my date, Emily Heart. Emily, this is Jake Miscoff; he runs the local banks, his wife, Merkel Miscoff, and an old friend of mine, Sarah Norman," he said, motioning to each of them.

The Miscoffs were dressed up as some sort of 1940s glamour couple, and I was pretty sure her diamond necklace was real. They were both older, with bits of gray in their hair, but they seemed spry and jolly. And then, there was Sarah. She was perfect.

Sarah was also dressed as a cat, like I was, only much more beautiful. Sequenced cat ears were tucked into her thick brown curls, and her outfit looked like a replica of the costumes they wore in *Cats*. And while one-pieces often made people look puffy, her costume perfectly hugged her natural hourglass figure. Her cat makeup looked like a mural on her face with glitter whiskers and a cute little pink nose. Beneath her thick eyelashes were a pair of light brown eyes that glowed with a hint of gold. She was smiling at me.

"It's wonderful to meet you, Emily," she said, extending her hand, "I feel so much better knowing I'm not the only cat here. I was afraid my costume was too generic, but seeing you here helped."

I shook her hand, and it was soft. "Well, mine is nothing like yours."

"If you mean not an embarrassing homemade one-piece, then you are right," she chuckled, "I think you look great."

"Well, thank you." I could feel my face turning red hot at the thought of someone as beautiful as her complimenting my looks.

"Sarah is a kindergarten teacher," John smiled.

"Yep," Sarah smiled back, "And I love every minute of it. What do you do, Emily?"

"Well, I was a secretary, but I'm out here visiting to take some time for myself to decide where I want to go from here. I just needed a change in scenery."

"That's how we met," John explained, giving me a wink, "She is staying at the B&B for the next few months. Best place to stay in town."

"Sure is," I grinned at him, admiring his attempt to promote the place like he had promised.

"Wait a second," interjected Jake Miscoff, "Heart? As in Robert and Mary Heart?"

My smile fell from my face, and my heart sank along with it.

"Are you their daughter?" his wife asked accusingly.

My throat was tight, and I couldn't speak. I simply nodded.

"Couldn't make it back for their funeral, and yet you have the gall to be here for your own selfish reasons, trying to escape the very place you left them here for? Disgusting," Jake huffed, shaking his head.

Sarah's mouth was agape, looking between the Miscoffs and me.

I could feel tears burning my eyes, but I was frozen in place. I couldn't move. John's hand was on my back, and he was whispering to me.

"Let's get out of here, Emily. Come on, I've got you," he hushed, guiding me out of the room. We pushed through the thick sea of people and out into the crisp night air, but I was still choking on the air like a drowned cat.

The car ride was a blur. John had taken me back to the B&B and sat me down at the kitchen table. Margaret was already asleep. He put the kettle on and set out two mugs with little teabags in them, pouring the hot water over the top and taking a seat beside me.

"I'm so sorry, Emily," he said, looking down at his mug.

I still hadn't spoken since we left the party.

"I won't ask anything; I know family can be complicated. Mine was. I had lived here with my parents, my brother, and my grandma, Margaret. She is my mom's mom. Anyway, my mom was always getting bruises on her, but we never saw her fall. We suspected it was my father, but since we never saw it happen, the police couldn't really do anything. And my mother always lied to him and covered it up. One day, he hurt her really bad, though, and my grandma drove her to the hospital, but there wasn't much they could do. She didn't make it. I was 12 at the time.

"My father wasn't there when we got home from the hospital, and we never saw him again, which was good. He easily could have turned on my grandmother or me. He wouldn't like who I am today, anyway. I haven't gone looking for him, and I don't plan to. I have Grams. My brother was devastated, though. He is a lot like our father, and we don't really talk anymore," he shrugged, taking a sip of his tea.

I held my mug close to me, feeling its warmth. I still didn't speak, but this time, it was for a different reason. I couldn't find the words to follow up his story. I put my mug back on the table and scooted my chair closer to John, laying my head on his shoulder. He wrapped his arm around me, and we sat like that for quite a while, in the silence of everything unsaid.

Once we finished our tea, we embraced each other, parted ways, and went to bed for the night.

Chapter 8

We all got into our own rhythms over the next week. John was usually busy with handiwork around the house, and Margaret was usually cooking, cleaning, or knitting in the living room. I spent much of my time walking around the trails that were scattered around town, winding through sparse neighborhoods full of wealthy houses and beautiful forests.

When he had the time, John would often sit down with me, bring me a warm drink, and we would share pleasantries. None of our conversations ever became too deep or revealing, not after the party. While opening up to someone usually creates a strong bond, for us it seemed to put up some sort of invisible glass wall between us.

When Tuesday rolled around, I worked up the mental courage to make plans to attend the local art class. I knew I needed to find myself again, and tracing my steps back to the things that made me happy before Hector came into my life sounded like a good place to start.

"Hey," John said, stopping me as I was on my out the door to class, "I was wondering if maybe you would like to have dinner with me tonight?"

I was a bit surprised by his question, and it took me a minute to answer, "Like a date?"

"Well, yeah," he smiled.

"Sure," I answered, although not really sure if I meant it or not, "I'm on my way to an art class, but when it's over I'll come back and change."

"Do you need a ride?"

"No. It's just at the elementary school down the street. It won't take but five minutes to walk. Thanks, though." I gave him a hug and stepped out the door.

When I arrived, there were already a few students there, sitting in metal chairs around a large round table. Most of them were older women, but there was one younger one who looked closer to my age. All of them had bags of supplies and were setting up their paper, pencils, paints, and brushes. I hadn't brought anything with me, so I decided to leave, feeling unprepared.

I didn't see the woman behind me as I stepped back out through the door and bumped right into her, making her drop her bag. I turned to see that it was Sarah, the woman from the party.

"I'm sorry," I pleaded, dropping to the ground to help her with her bag.

She kneeled down next to me, also reaching for her bag. Her hand grazed mine as we grasped the handle at the same time. An electric zing ran through my fingers. I looked up, catching the gaze of her golden eyes, which were framed by the little wrinkles of her bright smile.

"No problem, Emily," she assured, and we both stood up. "Are you here for the class?"

"I was, but I don't have any supplies," I shrugged.

"No problem, I always have extras. After class I'll give you a recommendation list for you to bring for next class. Come on in!"

I followed her into the classroom, where the students perked up immediately, all smiling and greeting her. I took the empty seat beside the younger woman. She didn't speak to me.

"Welcome, everyone! We have a new student today. Her name is Emily Heart. We are happy to have you! Now, since this month is Thanksgiving, I brought in a cornucopia with little pumpkins in it, and I figured we could have a practice today on still life drawing and painting," she said, cheerfully reaching into her bag.

She pulled out an old wicker cornucopia and placed it in the middle of the table, gently placing little pumpkins in it and a few around it as well. The other artists immediately got to work on their pieces, sketching and painting away in the echoing silence of the gymnasium. A few moments later, Sarah brought me some sketching paper, a sharpened pencil, and a fresh white eraser.

"Let me know if you need any help," she smiled, before walking around the room to look at the other students' progress.

I let out a sigh, relaxing as she stepped away, and I tried to focus on my drawing. I was relieved to find that drawing was much like riding a bicycle again. Although the first few marks were a bit messy, my hands were easily able to find their rhythm, and the image started to take form.

I scribbled in shading, smudged the lines with my fingertips, and cleaned up the edges with clean strokes from my eraser. It was like dancing, and soon, I was in a trance. My world was the paper, and I could create anything I wanted. I was in control.

"Great job, Emily," came the warm voice of Sarah over my shoulder.

I smiled, looking back over my shoulder at her. She smelled like coconuts and vanilla. My favorite.

"Thank you."

As she walked away, part of me wanted to stop her. To talk to her about something, or ask for her guidance on my work. She was so warm and she looked at me in a way that made me feel welcome.

The class whizzed by, and before I knew it, everyone was packing up and leaving while Sarah shouted out comments like 'Thanks for coming' and 'Be sure to tell your friends.'

I folded up my new picture and put it in my back pocket, then took the pencil and eraser up to Sarah.

"You are a great artist, Emily. I'm so glad to have you here with us," she said, taking the items and putting them in her bag.

"Glad to be here," I answered, turning to leave.

"Hey, Emily," she stopped me, "It's nice to meet another woman who isn't from around here. Well, I mean, since you just moved back here…Would you like to get a coffee sometime, and we can chat?"

I turned around, butterflies in my stomach. I didn't know why I was so nervous, "Yeah, I'd like that."

36

"Weekdays are pretty busy for me because of school. Are you free Friday night?"

"I am. Creekside Café?" I just couldn't seem to stop myself from blurting out the names of the places I knew in town. It wasn't very good for keeping my cover as a newcomer.

"Yep! 5:30?"

"Works for me," I agreed.

An awkward silence hung in the air for just a moment as we both stood there, just looking at one another. She really was beautiful, and I was excited to have a female friend in the area. Someone I could really relate to.

With a nod, I walked out of the room and back down the darkened street to the B&B. My walk wasn't as cold this time.

Chapter 9

"Ready," I said, skipping down the steps to meet John. He was already dressed up in black slacks and a formal evergreen sweater. It offset the dark red sweater dress I had picked up at the store on a whim earlier in the week.

"You seem extra cheery," he smiled, "Did you have a good time at the art class?"

"I did. It was so nice to draw again."

"Good," he opened the door and we went out to his car.

Honestly, I felt weird dating. I had just left my husband, and technically I was still married. I had never been one to just jump into another relationship. In fact, Hector had been my first, and only, real relationship. But that was my past, and I wanted so badly to forget it all and to move on with my life. And John was so sweet. Even though I didn't have feelings for him, I really did enjoy his company.

We pulled up to *Lorenzo's*, a small Italian bistro in town that had only just opened. The restaurant was a converted house off the main road. It had creaky wooden steps leading up to a cozy dining room that smelled of basil and garlic. The carpets were red, and the walls were decorated with paintings of the Italian countryside.

A waitress in a black dress with a dark brown pony tail, and almost too much makeup for her job title, showed us to a table by the window. The table was draped in a plain white tablecloth and had a small white tea light candle in the center. On either side of the candle were two laminated menus beside a pair of silverware which were wrapped in red napkins and two empty wine glasses.

"My name is Veronica; I will be your server tonight," she said, lighting the candle, "Let me know if you have any questions about our menu."

John and I took our seats, glancing over the list of food. It was basic Italian fare: various pastas, soups, salads, and pizzas. I placed my menu down, looking out the window into the darkness. My reflection looked pale.

"Everything alright?" John asked, reaching across the table to take my hand.

"Oh, um," I paused, looking down at our hands together, "Yes. I was just…thinking."

He sighed, taking his hand back and scooting his chair in. He placed his hands in his lap and took a deep breath. His face was softer now, but his lips buttoned together as if he were trying to hold back his words from escaping him.

"I know you don't think of me romantically, Emily," he started.

"John, it's not you. You are wonderful, it's just," I stuttered.

He held up his hand, silencing me before he continued, "I thought it was worth a shot. I've had a crush on you since we were little. No hard feelings, though. I am a strong believer in following one's heart. However, I need to tell you the real reason I brought you here tonight. I wanted to confide in you."

I settled into my chair, folding my hands under my chin as I leaned in. waiting to hear what he had to say. I was relieved and anxious all at the same time.

"I was both relieved and surprised when you didn't recognize me, Emily," he explained.

"I recognized your last name," I said, trying to cover up my confusion.

He smiled, "Yes. Well, when you knew me, I was a different person."

The waitress suddenly appeared beside our table, "Do you know what you would like to order? Can I start you off with drinks?"

"A bottle of the house merlot for the both of us and I'll have the chicken fettuccini alfredo," John answered, handing her his menu.

"And you, Miss?"

I hadn't really looked at the menu, "Same."

She smiled, taking my menu and scurrying away. I still had butterflies in my stomach as I looked over John's face, trying to find where I knew him from.

He gave a heavy sigh before continuing, "We had a few elementary classes together, and a high school math class the year before you moved away. But when you knew me, I wasn't John Wood. I was Jenny Wood."

I sat back in my seat, gazing back out the window, taking it all in. I looked back into his eyes and thought back to my memory of Jenny. The man in front of me was much different from the melancholy tomboy who sat next to me in math class. John was happy. John was a bright shining light. He was kind and warm, and I was lucky to have him.

I sighed with relief, a smile spreading across my face, "John, you look amazing, so happy now. That's why I didn't recognize you. And my distance isn't because of you or all the things you have confided in me about. It's just…"

"Your falling problem?" he interrupted

I nodded silently.

"Emily…"

Before he could continue, the waitress returned, filling our glasses with wine and setting the bottle on the table along with our meals.

"I'm sorry," he whispered. And we ate.

The food was hearty, and the wine was bittersweet. The meal, though, was silent. The mention of my bruises left me mute, and I don't think he knew what else to say.

The rest of the night was mostly a blur. When we arrived home, although we still hadn't spoken, John somehow seemed to know what was about to happen. I was still tipsy from the wine. Without a word, he enveloped me in his arms. There, in the darkness of the foyer, I pressed my face into the smell of sweet cologne on his scratchy sweater, and I cried. I just cried. I was finally crushed by the void in my chest. But peeking through the sadness in my tears was the realization that, for the first time in years, someone cared.

Chapter 10

Friday morning came around, and the day felt bright and new. After a few days of thinking over my dinner with John, I finally got the courage to pull out my laptop again. It was the first time I had opened my emails or looked at my accounts again.

The emails were a bit painful, but they were expected. I had a few emails from work officially telling me that I was fired for not showing up. I also had a few emails from Hector's family members feigning concern and expressing that I had hurt him deeply. Their messages were ended with their official corporation symbol and a digital signature. Even when attempting emotion, they were nothing but a cold corporate image.

But I wasn't ready for the messages that flooded my social media page. There were hundreds of new notifications on posts that included things like friends of my husband cussing me out, expressing their shock for my selfish behavior, and the worst of all, there were instant messages left for me by my husband:

Oct 30th:
Where are you?

Your phone went right to voicemail, how many times do I have to tell you to charge it...
Seriously, where the hell are you? We need you here at work.
Are you sick or something?
I'll send someone to check on you soon. You had better be sick as a dog if you miss work like this.
Thought you could just pack your bags and leave me?! You stupid bitch! You are nothing without me. I'll be here when you come crawling back like the piece of shit you are.

Oct 31st:
I'm sorry, baby. I know I get aggressive sometimes. That's why you left. I'll do better. Please come home.
So, you left your phone here, huh? I just found it.
You are just trying to piss me off.
You only have money because of me.

Nov 3rd:
Missed you at work today. The office is so lonely without you. Come home?

Nov 5th:
Your replacement came in today. She is so hot. Maybe it's good you left. Now, I can get what I deserve instead of settling for you.

Nov 8th:
You will regret leaving me.
Dumb cunt.
I will find you.

I slammed the computer shut and threw it across the room. I was shaking all over, and hot tears burned my eyes. I could feel my stomach tightening into knots. I ran down the hall to the bathroom, throwing the door open as I dry-heaved into the toilet. My whole body was convulsing, trying to force the pain out. Everything went fuzzy, and the next thing I knew, I was lying on the bathroom floor, looking up at the ceiling. My head was pounding. I had blacked out.

I picked myself up off the floor and wrapped a bathrobe around my shoulders for extra warmth. I then dragged myself back to my room and proceeded to pull myself together. I laid out the warmest outfit I had, which still wasn't much, as I hadn't bought a real coat yet. My light jackets and sweaters were meant for California, not the North East. I decided on a pink turtleneck and a pair of light-wash skinny jeans.
My hair was still a bit messy, but I didn't care. After a quick touchup with mascara and a little blush to mask the drained look on my face, I threw on the outfit and went downstairs to join everyone for breakfast. Margaret and John were already seated, and there was a pile of pancakes on a serving plate sitting in between them.

"Good morning," I said, trying to manage a smile. I could hear my voice crack.

"Good morning," Margaret said sweetly, "I made pancakes for breakfast. I think I made too many for us, but I wanted to practice making bigger meals since we will be getting new guests in a week."

"It looks wonderful, thank you."

"What are you up to today?" she asked.

I took a pancake from the pile, placing it on the plate in front of me, and smothering it in warmed syrup, "I think I am just going to take a taxi up to Greentown. I need some fresh air."

"That sounds like a wonderful idea," she smiled. John was silent, sipping his coffee and staring off into space. But he offered me a reassuring wink over his cup when he snapped out of it. I wondered what was on his mind.

"John, what are you doing today? Are you going with Emily?" Margaret asked, covering her own plate in pancakes and smothering them with butter.

"No," he replied, sitting back in his seat, "I'll just be doing a little bit of this and that. I was going to go through the cellar today and see if we have any decent Thanksgiving decorations. I still need to finish putting the rest of the Halloween decorations away."

At first, I was looking forward to a day by myself. I really needed some headspace to get myself together before having coffee with Sarah. But then I thought of myself alone on the trails in Greentown, and Hector's words rang in my mind...*I will find you.*

"Actually," I said, "I would love for you to come with me, John."
Margaret giggled.

"Alright," he smiled, taking another sip of coffee, "I do need to put the decorations away, though. Would you mind if I finished that before we go?"

"Take your time," I said, relaxing in my chair. The drive to Greentown was always breathtaking. It was only about 20 minutes away from Maple Creek, but the entire drive was completely made of rolling hills, winding roads, and towering trees. The town itself was extremely small, with only one main road and a few smaller roads leading off of it into residential neighborhoods.

In the center of the town was a small white church with a high-reaching steeple. It was the original church built in the town when it was first settled, and aside from a few updates, it was still in its original form.

Most of the houses were older as well, with many Victorian-style homes built in between the trees, which were mixed in with a few smaller cottages, most of which were well-kept. The cozy homes mixed with the bright fall leaves made the quiet town look more like an oil painting than a real-life place.

"Greentown was always my favorite place to visit this season," I sighed, looking out the car window as we turned down the main street of the town.

"It's very peaceful," John said.
John pulled the car into a parking spot on the main stretch. The street was lined on both sides with brick buildings that contained small businesses like clothing stores and flower shops. We got out of the car and started walking around aimlessly.

"Let's take a look in here," John said, pointing into one of the girly-looking clothes shops.

"Um, okay?"

He walked in a straight line to the back and immediately started rustling through one of the racks.

"See something you like?" I asked.

"I see something you'd like," he smirked, pulling a hanger off the rack. It was a bright red cold-weather coat with black fur lining on the inside. "You still need a coat."

"I love it! Great idea," I smiled, taking it from him and trying it on. It fits perfectly.

After I checked out with my coat, John and I continued our stroll. We bought a bouquet of daisies for Margaret and stopped at a small booth that was selling fresh apple cider. It was hot and spicy, and it helped fight the chilly air of the season. After we had passed all the shops in town, we took a turn down one of the residential streets and admired the beautiful little houses.

"Emily?" John asked.

"Yes?"

"I don't mean to pry, but I've been wanting to ask you…You showed up here with bruises and are going to be here for a few months…and you only use cash everywhere. Is there anything I can do for you?"

I felt my body tighten up at his questions, but after a pause, I decided to answer, "Thanks, John. I'm alright. I've been avoiding talking about it because it's just so painful, and I haven't really wrapped my head around it yet. I was…I mean, I am…married to Hector Jacobson. I've been saving up money for a year to leave him because I was tired of being scared all the time. We had one of our usual fights, and the next morning, when he went to work early, I simply packed my bags and left."

John stopped, looking away for a moment. The house we had stopped in front of was a small stone and white wood cottage with a fenced in garden which was full of overgrown rose bushes. Beside the mailbox read a sign that said "For Sale."

"I'm sorry," he said, looking over at me with a sense of sincere concern.

"I'm alright, or at least I will be. It doesn't hurt as much as I expected. It's just strange. I haven't been alone in years."

"You aren't alone," he said, giving me a nudge. After a pause, his tone lightened up again, "This would be a nice place to settle down, huh?" He pointed to the house.

"It looks like a fairytale. But I don't have a job right now, and I don't know if I could afford it." John shrugged, "Well, if fairytales teach us anything, then anything can happen."

I couldn't help but smile, "I almost forgot, what time is it?"

"It's just past noon," he said, checking the time on his phone, "Why do we need to be back at a certain time for one of your art classes or something?"

"Kind of," I said, putting my hands in my coat pockets.

"Oh?"

"I'm having coffee with Sarah tonight," I shrugged.

A strange sort of smile spread across his face, and I couldn't quite place his reaction, "Well then, I will be sure to have us back in time for that. Sarah really is a great person. She is so…"

"Beautiful," I finished his sentence.
He nodded, "Beautiful."

After another hour or so of wandering and joking about our old schools and memories, we got back in the car and headed back to the B&B. I couldn't stop the butterflies the whole ride back. I hadn't been that excited about something in a long while. But it was just a cup of coffee, or at least that's what I kept telling myself.

Chapter 11

I considered touching up my makeup a little before heading out to meet Sarah, but I decided against it. I felt ridiculous after the thought crossed my mind. She would have been coming from work, and what kind of woman would get dolled up to have coffee with another woman?

I left about half an hour before our meeting time, just to be sure I wouldn't be late since I decided to walk. It was just a little too close to the B&B to get a ride. I arrived early, and she still wasn't there, so I took a seat at one of the tiny round tables in the corner of the café.

There were about a dozen similar tables for two all crammed into a room that really should have only been able to comfortably fit about half of them. The theme was a mix between 'brown' and 'randomly placed potted plants.' There were large ferns by the door, hanging plants in the corners of the room, and a baby cactus by the register. The tables and chairs were all brown, and the clock on the wall behind the cash register was in the shape of a white coffee cup.

Sarah walked into the coffee shop a few minutes later with all the grace of a small-town Audrey Hepburn. Her dark curls were wrapped in a loose bun atop her head, and she wore a casual black coat over a pair of gray slacks and an artistic floral scarf. She wore barely any makeup, but she didn't even need the little bit she had on. She glowed.

Upon seeing me, she waved and weaved through the jungle of chairs, dropping her purse from her shoulder and taking the seat across from me.

"Hey, Emily! Nice coat, I love it," she grinned.

"Oh, thank you."

"Have you ordered anything yet?"

"Not yet."

"Well, is it cliché if I say I'm probably getting a pumpkin spice latte?" she giggled.

"Not at all. I love those, too," I smiled back.

"Great! I'll grab us two."

"Oh, you don't have to pay for mine."

"I want to," she said with a wink.

I felt a flutter in my chest. She walked over to order our drinks, and I took a deep breath and looked down at my lap. I tried to gather my thoughts, but before I could, she was sitting down in front of me again with a little plastic number 14 that she sat on the edge of the table.

"So, what brought you back to Maple Creek?" she asked, her wide smile still lighting up her face.

"Oh," I paused, tucking my hair behind my ear, "I grew up here, actually. But I had been living out in California for the last few years. I guess I missed it."

"Maybe you could show me a few things then," she said, "I only moved here about three years ago."

"I'd like that," I responded, and I could feel a blush lighting up my cheeks, "So what brought you here, then?"

"Well, I'm actually from an even smaller town than this, believe it or not. It's called Oaktonville. It's about an hour north of here. Anyway, I went to school to be a kindergarten teacher like I always dreamed of, and I was convinced I was going to teach at the elementary school in Oaktonville. But my family and I haven't always seen eye to eye, and when I was looking at job postings in the area, I saw this one available. I needed a breath of fresh air, and this was it."

"I can understand that."

One of the baristas nudged his way past the chairs with our coffees and placed them on the table, taking our number without a word, and returned to the register. His expression was blank, and ironically he seemed like he could use a cup of coffee.

Sarah cupped her coffee in both hands, inhaling deeply, "Mmm, yummy."

She was so cute. There was a silence while we each took a few scalding hot sips of our drinks. I set my coffee down, looking up and catching her eye. She smiled with a sigh, and my cheeks turned warmer than my latte.

"Um," I started, clearing my throat, "So what got you into teaching art to adults if your passion is kindergarten?"

"It's always been a hobby of mine, and I needed extra money," she shrugged, taking another sip of her coffee.

A bit of foam escaped the lid of her cup and gave her a little mustache of bubbles. She licked it off slowly from her soft pink lips, and I couldn't help but wonder if she would taste like pumpkin spice. I shook my head, going back to focusing on my own coffee. I felt crazy. I had never thought like that about another girl, and I had to hook my ankles around the legs of my chair to stop myself from springing up from my seat and bolting out the door.

"And speaking of art, you are a great artist," she said.

"Thanks. I used to do it daily, but it just sort of faded away from my life over time. I was excited when I saw the flier for your class. I've been wanting to get back into it."

"Well, I'm so very glad you came."

I could feel the butterflies returning to my stomach, and I suddenly found myself standing up from my seat.

"Are you okay?" she asked.

"Oh, um, yes. I just have…a headache. My head is starting to hurt. I think I better go home and lay down before it gets too bad."

Her smile dropped, and I felt my heart sink, too.

"Do you need a ride or anything?" she asked.

"That's okay. The fresh air will do me some good," I said starting to make a bee line for the door with my coffee in hand. As I my hand touched the handle I looked back with the biggest smile I could muster, "Sarah?"

She spun around in her chair, "Yes?"

"I had a wonderful time. I'll see you at art class in a few days. Thank you so much for the coffee." Her smile returned, "I look forward to it. Anytime, Emily. I hope we can do this again sometime." I nodded and walked out the door, my gaze up towards the moon that was already showing up in the sky. It was a beautiful evening, and I knew I wouldn't be getting much sleep. I had a lot to think about.

Chapter 12

I spent the few days between the coffee meeting with Sarah and the next art class lying in bed and searching my thoughts for the answers on what to do next. I even considered praying to God a few times, but decided against it. I wasn't fully sure what exactly it was that I was trying to figure out.

Was I having some weird mental breakdown because of the stress I was under? Was I a lesbian, a bisexual, or whatever I would have been called? Or perhaps I was thinking about it all wrong, and I did just want to be friends with her, and my brain was simply admiring her beauty and her friendship.

I stared up at the blank white ceiling while memories flashed in front of my eyes like movie scenes being projected on the white sheet of a drive-in movie theater. I saw Hector raising his hand to me for the first time. I saw myself crying on the bathroom floor with a knife in my hand. I saw myself forcing a smile on our coworkers when they gushed over what a lovely couple we were at the company parties. But clearer than all the other images, I also saw myself boarding that plane.

I had left my old life of pain in search of one filled with hope and happiness. And although it hadn't been with the vision of finding someone to love, I knew one thing for certain: Sarah made me happy. Just the thought of her smile lifted a weight from my chest, and

I melted into the bed. I didn't know if she felt the same, but I knew I had to at least try. I wasn't attracted to Sarah because she was a woman but because she made me feel more like a woman.

I threw the covers off of myself, finally feeling energized again at the thought of the art class that evening. I picked out a black V-neck sweater and a pair of jeans. I even threw on a tiny pair of diamond earrings. I practically flew down the steps to join Margaret and John for dinner before class. I was starving.

"It's alive!" John chuckled over a sandwich.

"Oh, good. I was getting worried. You were so quiet all weekend, Emily. Would you like a sandwich as well?" Margaret asked.

"Yes, please," I answered, taking a seat across from John. Margaret disappeared into the kitchen.

"You are looking chipper today," John commented, raising an eyebrow.

"Art class tonight," I shrugged.

"Oooh," John winked.

"Iced tea?" Margaret asked, bringing in a thick, neat sandwich on a paper plate and setting down an empty glass.

"Sounds good," I answered. She hurried back into the kitchen and came out with a pitcher, filling my cup.

"Now," she started, taking a seat beside me, "John was telling me you might have plans to move back here permanently?"

"Yes, it's one of the decisions I am working on making over the next few months. Also, I'm sorry I didn't recognize you, Miss Margaret."

"Don't worry about it, dear. I only saw you once at a school function. But it was John that actually reminded me who you were and that you had grown up together. Now, onto you moving here. Have you thought about where you might want to work?"

"I'm not really sure. My only real experience is as a secretary, but with this being a small town, I'm not sure how many positions like that would be available," I said, taking a sip of my tea.

"Well, I'll keep on the lookout for you then. We would love to have you stay here in town. You have been a blessing for John. He hasn't smiled this much in a while. He has really needed a friend," she said, standing and going back into the kitchen.

"And what are you doing today, John?" I asked.

"Oh, just fixing this and that. Getting everything ready for the new people. And, speaking of things that will be happening soon, I am going to a play at the school next week. Would you like to go?"

"Sure, sounds like fun."

He nodded and went back to finishing his sandwich. The rest of the afternoon passed quickly. I did some laundry, picked up my room, and tried to keep busy until it was time to go. I made sure to leave a few minutes early so that I could walk around the block to ease my nerves on the way to class.

The class had the same students as the last one did. And this time, I had brought some paper and pencils of my own. Not even a minute after I took my seat, Sarah burst through the door to the gym. She had a bulky black duffle bag slung over her shoulder and the thick curls of her hair were pulled back into a messy ponytail. Her mascara was a bit smudged and she was panting a bit as if she had literally run to class.

"Hey guys!" she huffed, "Sorry, I'm a bit later than usual. But I have a really cool surprise for you today. I know we always do drawing and painting, but I brought some supplies today so we can shake things up a bit. We are going to try sculpting! Specifically, we are each going to sculpt a tree."

"A big tree?" one of the older ladies asked, squinting at Sarah through her purple glasses.

"No," laughed Sarah, "A small tree. I've brought pieces of cardboard to build them on, some wire and popsicle sticks for support, and polymer clay to build them." She unpacked each of the items onto the table and explained, "Oh, and here is a bag of bright fall leaves. I picked them up from outside. I thought it would add a nice natural touch if our trees had seasonal leaves on them."

"This sounds silly," the older lady grumbled. Sarah's shoulders sank a bit, and the room fell silent for a moment.

"Well, I think it's beautiful. I'd love a little fall tree sculpture in my room," I assured her, standing up and grabbing a handful of supplies.

Her face softened, and she perked up a bit. The rest of the students followed along and grabbed some supplies of their own. Within a few minutes, everyone was working on their trees.

I made the skeleton of the tree with wire, giving it long roots to stand on The trunk was made of wire wrapped around some popsicle sticks, and the end of the metal wire reached up to create branches. I unwrapped a rectangle block of grey clay, and began trying to mold it. It was hard as a rock. After a few minutes of wrestling with it, I saw Sarah make her way over to me.

"Here," she said, taking the block from me, "Start with smaller pieces. And sometimes it just needs a little warmth to soften up."

She tore off a corner of the clay and rubbed it in her hands, her thumb pressing into it as it softened. She then placed the clay onto the base of my tree trunk and gently took my hand, helping to guide my fingers as we formed the clay around the wire to make the trunk. An electric buzz ran through my hands as she laid her hands over mine, and I had to stop myself from entwining my fingers with hers.

"See?" she asked, pulling away, "Just like that." With a wink, she turned and made her way back around the table to help another student.

Part of me thought I had imagined the wink. Women didn't often wink at each other, or at least, they didn't usually wink at me. And yet, there I was, with Sarah. I tried to convince myself that maybe she just saw me as a friend, to try and slow my heart from beating out of my chest when I looked up at her. But I knew there was definitely something more. There had to be.

My tree built up, layer by layer until all the popsicle sticks and wires were hidden underneath its clay bark. I didn't have enough time to put on the leaves or to paint it, but Sarah assured us that we would have time to finish our art the next week, just before Thanksgiving.

The room of people packed up silently. I took my time to make sure that I would have a moment alone with Sarah on the way out. I really wanted to talk to her about how I was feeling. I left my statue and sketching supplies neatly piled in my spot and walked up beside her as she finished packing her duffle bag.

"Thanks for coming to another class, Emily," Sarah smiled, slinging her bag over her shoulder.

"I like getting to spend time with you," I answered, butterflies fluttering in my stomach. I could barely breathe.

"You're too kind," she said.

"It's just the truth," I replied, "I think you're…" the words caught in my throat, "I think you're beautiful."

I could feel my heart beating away, but it felt like there was a magnet pulling me towards her, and even my fear couldn't stop it. I took a small step forward, leaned in, and kissed her soft pink lips. She tasted just as sweet as I had imagined.

Neither of us moved for a moment, and I stepped back again to see her reaction. Her face was blank and emotionless. She looked at me like we were strangers, and her fingers came up to brush against her lips. Without a word, she turned away from me and walked out of the gym.

My heart stopped its wild beating, and my breath slowed down. I stood alone in the big, empty gymnasium. A single tear streaked my cheek as I collected my things and walked back to the B&B. *What had I done?* I asked myself. It was the only thing on my mind all night. I didn't sleep.

Chapter 13

I spent the week leading up to the play helping out around the Bed and Breakfast and running errands with John. It was nice to have the distractions of work, and spending time with John was always fun. He tried to bring up Sarah a few times, but I was able to brush it off by asking more questions about whatever project we were working on.

John taught me how to fix light sockets that weren't working, the kind of light bulbs that needed to be used in each of the rooms, how to unclog the sinks and toilets without messing up the fragile plumbing of the old house, and he even taught me how to make his homemade apple cider. By the end of the week, I was practically his apprentice. I didn't go back to class to finish my tree that week.

The play was on a Wednesday night, which I thought was a little strange. He hadn't told me what we were seeing, but based on his excitement in trying to get us out the door on time and emphasizing how important it was to get good parking, I imagined there was some sort of fancy community theater in town that I was unaware of.

He said to dress casually, so to combat the frigid weather, I layered a sleeved shirt with my pink hoodie and my new red jacket with a matching pair of knitted black gloves, as well as a hat that I had picked up on one of my shopping runs with John. He was layered in much the same way I was in browns and greys. The whole way there, he had a bright smile on his face, like a kid on his way to see Santa. I was really curious about what we were going to see, but I decided not to ask and to simply let it be a surprise.

I was shocked to see that, as we drove down Main Street, the car didn't continue on through town, and instead, John turned on his blinker and pulled us into the parking lot of the elementary school.

"The play is at the elementary school?" I asked, trying not to sound panicked.

"Yeah," he chuckled, "They always put on a fall play before Thanksgiving break. My niece is in it. She's in 2nd grade this year."

"I didn't know you had a niece. It's sweet that you go to see her."

"Yeah, she is great. I go every year. She always makes me promise to go. But I don't talk about her often because my brother and I don't get along, and so I don't see her much."

The parking lot was overflowing, but we were lucky enough to drive up on someone as they pulled out of a spot in the second row. The sky was grey and threatening rain as we followed the small crowd into the auditorium. There were a lot more people there than I would have expected for an elementary school play. At least 100 adults filled the movie theater-style seats. Some more sat in metal folding chairs near the back, and others stood around the walls. The whole room was buzzing with the hum of chit-chat.

"Over here. Let's stand in the back so we can get some pictures when she comes on," John said, finding us a spot near the painted cement wall by the door.

We arrived just in time, because only a few minutes later, the lights dimmed and the play started. Classes of students were brought on one at a time to do a little song, dance, or skit that related to fall. There was an older woman, who I assumed was the music teacher, playing a piano on the side of the stage to accompany their performances.

We saw a class of little dancing leaves, a skit about a turkey and his farmer friend that turned into a class sing-a-long of Old McDonald, and then there was a song about cozy sweaters. Then, John perked up as a group of students came onstage dressed in normal school clothes.

"There she is," he whispered, taking out his phone and setting it to record.

His niece was wearing a blue striped long-sleeve shirt, and she had long golden blonde hair that was pulled back into a ponytail. She looked to be about seven or eight years old. Her class put on a short skit about a class going on a field trip to a pumpkin patch. One of the students was teased for being too weak to carry their pumpkin, but then the character played by his niece came over to help, and they became friends. It was actually pretty cute.

Once they got off stage, the final group came on. It was the kindergarten class, and they were all dressed up as pumpkins. It took all my will not to run out the door in awkward embarrassment when Sarah came on stage with them to help them with their dance. She was matching them in a pumpkin shirt, and her hair was down, allowing her curls to bounce as she danced and wiggled along with her students. Her eyes sparkled up there as she laughed and giggled with her little pumpkins. She looked really happy.

When they finished, they all skipped off, holding hands and waving, and the lights came back on again. A lot of the parents stood from their seats with bouquets of flowers and mingled together, talking and laughing while they waited for their kids to come out from backstage.

"So, what did you think?" John asked.

"It was adorable. Your niece seems really sweet," I smiled.

"She is. I want to wait for her so we can say hi, and then we can get going."

"No rush."

I scanned the room, part of me hoping I would see Sarah, and another part of me dreading the idea. I decided to stay behind John so there would be less of a chance of her seeing me first.

"Oh, there is my brother," John said, starting to move towards the front of the crowd, "And here comes Alice."

"Uncle John!" Alice squealed, running up and jumping into John's arms. He spun her around and put her down again, kneeling down in front of her, "You came! Did you see me up there?"

"I did, Alice. You did so well," he said, grinning from ear to ear.

Within seconds, his brother was behind him, pulling him up by his jacket, "What did I say about staying away from my daughter?"

His brother had the outward appearance of a family man, with the typical haircut, and the polo shirt tucked into a pair of jeans and an all-weather jacket. But there was a look in his eyes and a tone his voice that hinted that there was something darker in him.

"I promised her I'd come. I just wanted her to know I was here, and now we'll be going," John said, brushing his brother's hand off his shoulder.

"We?" his brother asked, looking over at me, "What is this? Your girlfriend? You know he's not really a man, right?"

"Come on, John, let's go," I said, taking his hand.

His brother continued his mocking, laughing loud enough to draw the attention of the nearby parents, "Ugh, you have this woman convinced you are a man. That is hilarious."

I could feel my temper rising, and my face turned red hot as I snatched my hand from John and got in his brother's face, yelling, "He is more of a man than you!"

"Excuse me?" his brother asked, puffing up his chest.

His wife took Alice's hand and led her out of the auditorium. I had a feeling this wasn't the first time he had acted like this in public. My hands were shaking. I didn't know what had come over me, but I was even more unsure about how to get out of what I had started. I felt his brother step closer, getting within an inch of me. His face was bright red as he started screaming something incoherent.

Everything happened in slow motion, like in the movies. I looked over his shoulder to see Sarah looking at me from a few rows over. Her eyes were watery, and her lips were turned down into a frown as she locked eyes with me. The next thing I knew, the brother's hand grabbed my jacket, and John's hand was on my shoulder. He threw me backward, and I landed with a slap on the hard tile ground, running into a few people as I did. I looked up to see John and his brother latched onto each other, snarling like animals.

John's brother, who was much larger than him, put his hands on his shoulders, picked him up by his jacket again, and threw him onto the ground. John's head bounced off the tile, and I wanted so badly to rush over to him and help somehow. But I'd never seen a fight like this, and I was paralyzed with fear.

His brother got on top of him, beating his face with his big, meaty fists. John threw his arms up to protect himself but with little success. A few of the other fathers in the crowd rushed over and pulled his brother off of him, and I was able to crawl over to help John.

I laid his head in my lap and brushed his hair back, "John, can you hear me? John?" I asked frantically. His face was all puffed up, and blood ran from his mouth and nose. He was unconscious. "Someone call 9-1-1!"

John's brother shook off the people holding him, spat at John, and walked out the door, muttering,

"You fight like a girl. Maybe because you are one loser."

Chapter 14

The dull beeps on the monitor filled the silence of the hospital room. I sat beside John, clutching the arms of a chair as I waited for Margaret to arrive. He was hooked up to a bunch of lines, and he was dressed in a green hospital gown and lightly covered in a white sheet from the waist down.

I had the hospital call the B&B to let her know what happened. I hadn't eaten dinner yet, and the neon lights were giving me a headache, but I wanted to be there with him in case he woke up, or at least until the doctors had more information on his condition.

After about half an hour of sitting there, one of the nurses came into the room, "You have a visitor in the waiting room, should I bring them in?"

"Yes, please," I said anxiously.

She left again and a few more minutes passed before she came back again. I stood and crossed the room to hug Margaret, only, it wasn't her. It was Sarah. She rushed into the room and threw her arms around me.

"I'm so glad you are okay. I thought you were going to be in that fight. Has John woken up yet? Is he going to be alright?" Her words ran together, and I could feel her shaking.

I took a step back and looked her over. She was shattered into pieces. I tried to reassure her. "He hasn't woken up yet, and I'm still waiting to hear back from the doctor."

She walked over to the bedside and held his hand. My head was spinning. She was acting as if the last time I'd seen her had never happened. As if our kiss hadn't happened. I wanted to explain myself and apologize, but she didn't bring it up.

"Sarah," I said, taking a step closer to her, "Can I talk to you for a minute?"

She turned to face me, teary-eyed. I knew this probably wasn't a good time, with all of us worried about John. But this had been weighing on me for over a week.

"Sarah, I'm sorry about kissing you the other day. I know it was weird. I don't know what came over me. That's why I missed the last art class, too. I just felt bad," I explained,

She stepped closer to me, and my heart skipped as she reached down to take my hand and whispered, "I wanted you to kiss me."

"But you left," I said, taking my hand back.

"Where is he? Is he okay? Where's my Johnny?" came Margaret's voice as she pushed through the door into the room.

I rushed over to hug her, and we stood there for a minute, just embracing each other. Luckily, we didn't have to wait long for the answers to her question, as the doctor came in shortly after she did.

"Hello, my name is Dr. Scott," explained a man who looked almost too young to be a doctor, "I apologize for taking so long, but I wanted to wait for all his scans to come back before I talked to you. We had a CAT scan and an x-ray done of his head and shoulders. The good news is that he has no spinal damage to his neck. He does, however, have a mild concussion, a few fractures on his cheekbone and jaw, as well as a broken nose, and some lacerations in his mouth from his teeth."

"How bad are the fractures? Is he going to have to stay in the hospital?" asked Margaret frantically.

"Who are you to the young man?" Dr. Scott asked, looking over the chart.

"I'm Margaret Davies, his Grandmother. He lives with me."

"Okay, well then, I will be sure to give you a packet of care information when he goes home. They are just hairline fractures, but we don't want them to get worse. We will keep him overnight to monitor his concussion. He should be waking up soon, and once he does, we will run a few more tests. He should be free to go home tomorrow. He will need a lot of rest and ice and probably someone to take full care of him for a while."

"How long to recover?" I jumped in.

"He should start feeling much better in 2-3 weeks," Dr. Scott explained, opening the door to leave.

"Thank you, doctor," Margaret sighed, going to John's side.

"Can I talk to you for a moment in the hall?" Sarah asked, breaking the silence that followed the doctor's departure.

I nodded, following her into the fairly busy hallway. Nurses ran here and there in bright-colored scrubs, and there was a constant beeping from the various monitors near the nurse's station. Sarah looked around nervously.

"I have something to tell you, and I've only said this out loud to a few people ever in my life," she explained in a whisper, leaning in close to me. "I'm...I'm a lesbian."

She tucked a stray curl behind her ear. My heart leaped with joy from my chest. I was terrified that I had been acting like some kind of freak, kissing another girl. It was all so new to me. But here she was, another woman who felt the same way I did. I wasn't alone.

A huge smile spread across my face, and I took her hand. But she quickly pulled it away, and my heart sank again.

"Not in public. Not here. People might see," she explained, "I'm not out to everyone. That's why I left when you kissed me. I got scared. I was afraid my students might come back in and see us or something."

I nodded, but I didn't fully understand. Here I was with this beautiful woman, and I could feel that warm, bubbly happiness dancing around inside of me, and yet, I couldn't express it. I couldn't touch her.

"I do want to spend some time with you, though," she assured me, "I know this is kind of a bad time with what happened to John. He's been a good friend of mine. Once he is starting to feel better, maybe sometime next week, you could come by my place? I was going to be putting up my Christmas lights and decorating the house. I can make dinner. Should I text you the address?"

"That sounds wonderful. But my phone is broken," I lied.

"Okay, well, John and Margaret know my address. You can get it from them. I'm excited to see you. Tell John I was here when he woke up. I'll come over to the B&B to check on him in a few days. I've got to get going back to the school to finish helping clean up from the performance. See you soon?"

"Yeah, I look forward to it," I smiled.

I went back into the room, my chest fluttering still from her smile. But the feeling washed away like I was hit by a splash of cold water, and I came back to reality. Moments after I entered the room, John started to stir and blink awake.

"John!" Margaret and I cried in synchronicity, both of us lunging towards him.

"Grams?" he asked in a hoarse voice.

"I'm here, baby!" she assured, taking his hand and sitting in bed beside him.

"Where's Emily?" he asked, wincing as he tried to sit up.

"I'm here," I said, standing opposite Margaret.

"Lay back down, hun," she said, "You need to rest. The doctors want to keep you here until tomorrow just to make sure your concussion isn't too bad. You have a couple of fractures, but you will be okay in a month or so."

"But what about work?" he asked, laying back again.

"We will figure that out later. Right now you rest."

"Are you okay, Emily? He didn't hurt you, right?" John asked, turning to face me.

"I'm just fine. And Sarah was here to see you earlier, but she had to leave. She said she will come and visit in a few days."

73

"Did she, now?" he said with a little smirk followed by another wince.

"What?" I asked, "She is worried about you. She really likes you, John."

He chuckled a bit, "She really likes you, too, Emily."

I could feel my face flush as I looked over at Margaret to see if she had caught it. She looked up at me with a wink, and I assumed John had mentioned a thing or two to her. But before I had too much time to think about it, the nurse came in again.

"Margaret Davies?" she asked

"That's me," Margaret replied, standing from the hospital bed and crossing the room to stand by the nurse.

"Can I talk to you for a moment in private?" the nurse asked. She had long dark hair and glammed up makeup that matched her bright purple scrubs. But even with her colorful look, her face was grim. I could tell there was something wrong in the way her mouth was turned down, and her eyebrows scrunched together.

"You can speak in front of all of us," John said, "Anything that has to do with my care concerns everyone here."

"Um, okay. Well, the doctor wanted me to give you some paperwork and send you home now."

"Home? Doesn't he need to be moved out of the ER to a room here? The doctor said they would be keeping him overnight," Margaret asked frantically.

"Well, the doctor thinks that *she*," the nurse stressed the word, looking past both of us to John, "is fine enough to be monitored from home. The scans didn't show any sort of major trauma aside from the minor fractures, so you guys can take her home and watch her there. The paperwork includes care information and what to look for if you need further medical assistance. Dr. Scott has called one of the doctors at the hospital in Harvest, and they said they are willing to take care of you guys if you need anything from here on out."

"Harvest?!" Margaret exclaimed, "That's over two hours away! Does he need a specialist or something?"

"No, it's just that Dr. Scott was unaware that John is a woman. Once the nurses informed him, he felt uncomfortable with any further treatment. It would go against his religion to treat her since being transgender goes against God," the nurse explained, handing Margaret some paperwork and taking over a release form to John and having him sign it.

"Are you kidding me? You stupid backward hicks! This is a hospital, and my grandson is hurt. How dare you…"

"Grams," John interrupted, "It's okay. Harvest is a great hospital. Remember? That's where I got my hormone therapy done. I like them a lot better anyway."

"But, John!" Margaret begged, her face turning red.

"It's okay," he nodded.

The nurse unhooked John from his monitors and scurried out of the room without another word.

"How did they know you were a woman?" I asked John, helping him sit up so we could get him dressed.

"I haven't had my surgery yet. Still saving up the money," he said.

The left side of his face was like a puffy red and purple balloon, but he was in good spirits. We got him dressed in his clothes, which were still speckled in blood from the fight. Then, all three of us went out to Margaret's car, which was a small, newer-looking tan car. John's car was still at the school, and I rode in the ambulance with him to the hospital.

John sat in the passenger seat, and I sat in the back on the cool leather bench. Everyone was silent on the way back.

Chapter 15

The new tenants arrived the next morning: Thanksgiving Day. They were an Asian family who had come to visit local relatives who had moved to America a few years before. The family was an older couple with their 20-something daughter. They didn't speak much English, but they were kind and laughed a lot, which helped lighten up the energy in the house.

I spent most of the day tending to John. I helped him stand when he needed to, I fed him soft snacks that I snuck from the kitchen, and I made sure he was always on time for taking his double dose of over-the-counter pain medication. Margaret was cooking up a storm all day, but the few times I went down, it appeared that the new family was helping her out in the kitchen, so I didn't worry too much about her. They all seemed to be enjoying themselves.

And I was enjoying myself in my own way, as well. Even injured, John was cheery. To avoid boredom from his bedrest, he sent me to the basement to rummage through old dusty boxes where I found some decks of cards, and we sat together on his bed playing various card games and enjoying the day.

By the late afternoon, Margaret was calling us down for dinner, and I helped John dress in a suit and tie. I then went to my room, threw on a pair of black leggings and a tan sweater dress, and went back to help John down the stairs. He was greeted by everyone with cheers and hugs, and then I helped him to his seat and poured him some cider.

The table was absolutely overflowing with food and drinks. In the center of the table was a giant honey-glazed turkey, which was surrounded by plates of salads, berries, nuts, and pies. The entire room had a warm glow about it.

"While I cut the turkey, let's each go around and say something we are thankful for this year," said Margaret, picking up a carving knife and pulling the turkey closer to herself. "I'm grateful for my grandson, John. And I am grateful that he is going to heal up just fine."

Everyone clapped.

"I am grateful for my Grams, for my newest friend, Emily, and for being able to be here today with all of you," said John with a glance across the table to the young Asian woman. She seemed to notice, and they locked eyes for a moment, and I couldn't help but smile as I looked back and forth between them.

I cleared my throat, "And I am grateful for the wonderful people I have met here and for the fresh start I am getting here in Maple Creek."

"I am grateful for the family we are visiting here and for America as their new home," the older man said, nodding to each of us. "We will be going over to have a meal with them after we eat some here."

"I grateful for family," the wife said in a thick accent, taking his hand and then looking at her daughter.

The daughter remained silent, and her gaze returned to John. Her mother muttered something to her and gestured at us.

"I am grateful for the food and for your hospitality. Thank you," the daughter said, smiling at each of us.

"You are very welcome. We are so glad to have you here. We hope you enjoy your stay," said Margaret, placing some turkey on each of our plates.

Only a few bites into the delicious food, the front door was suddenly swung open and slammed shut. We all paused, turning to see who had come in, and Margaret stood from her seat, preparing to greet them.

"Happy Thanksgiving!" squeaked Sarah, taking off her knitted winter hat, revealing a mess of curls that fell into her face and draped down her shoulders. "It's freezing out there. Brrr!"

"Sarah!" exclaimed Margaret, "Come join us. Take a seat."

"Thanks," she said, going for the seat across from me.

John threw back his chair and stood, wobbling a bit as he did, "Sarah, here, take my seat so you and Emily can chat about art and stuff. I'll take the other seat." His words were a bit slurred through the puffiness of his face.

"Are you sure?" she asked hesitantly.

"Of course!"

"Okay, thanks," she said, sitting in the chair beside me and scooting it in. She smelled like vanilla sugar. "And how are you doing, John? It's only been a day, but the swelling looks like it's already going down a bit."

"Has it?" he asked, taking the seat across from us beside the young woman, "I have been avoiding mirrors. But I've been feeling better, thanks for asking. Emily has been taking great care of me. And we have some wonderful new company as well."

John looked beside him at the young woman who smiled into her lap at his glance. Most women I knew would have been nervous or uncomfortable around a man with a bruised face, but she didn't seem to mind.

Everyone dug into the scrumptious piles of food. I filled my plate with berries, stuffing, and a large slice of pumpkin pie that I laid alongside my piece of turkey Margaret had given me.

I took my first bite of turkey. It was seasoned perfectly, juicy, and warm. And just as I reached over to my cup to take a sip of my cider, I felt a hand on my lap. It was Sarah's hand. I looked over at her, and she was just going on, eating her food as if nothing was happening. My eyes darted around the table to see if anyone else had noticed or was freaking out, but they were all just eating and conversing casually.

79

Her hand slid up my thigh, and I could feel my legs quiver, and part of me wanted to push her away. *Didn't you want this? For her to like you back?* I thought to myself.

I held my breath, looking back to Sarah. Her eyes had those little lines around them when she smiled. A soft crease framed her lips. She was perfect.

I reached down with my hand, and instead of pushing her away, I laid my hand on hers, intertwining our fingers. Her hand fit perfectly in mine, and a sense calm washed over me. I breathed a sigh of relief as I settled back into my chair, and joined in on the conversation with the rest of the group. The food was delicious and filling; the best I had ever had.

Once everyone was done eating, the young woman sat to keep John company while her parents helped Margaret take dishes to the kitchen. Sarah and John shared pleasantries and a hug goodbye before I walked her to the door.

"Glad to see he is doing well," she commented as she put her hat back on.

"Yeah, he is strong and seems to find the best in everything. I admire that about him," I smiled.

"We still on for decorating next week?" she asked.

"Of course. I can't wait."

She looked over my shoulder, and I looked behind me as well, but I didn't see anyone there. When I turned back to her, she gave me a quick kiss on the cheek and skipped out the door. I watched her walk down to her car and then close the door with a quiet click.

I considered going to the kitchen to help Margaret, but as I walked past the dining room, I caught a quick glimpse of John and the young woman out of the corner of my eye. Sarah's kiss on my cheek wasn't the only one stolen that Thanksgiving. I decided to give them their space and, instead, retired to my room to lie down and think about what I was going to do about Sarah.

How could I tell Sarah I was married?

Chapter 16

A week passed, and with John not only starting to feel better but also having Kiuchi, the young woman who was staying with us, taking care of him now, I decided it was time to go see Sarah.

I dressed in my red sweater with a pair of jeans and my red coat thrown over it. I put a black clip in my hair to keep it out of my face and applied a little more makeup than usual. I wanted to look nice but not like I was trying too hard. Although, part of me thought that by putting that much thought into it, I was already trying too hard.

I went downstairs to get the address from Margaret, who was dusting around the living room. I slipped on my jacket and some snow boots as I did.

"Hey, do you have Sarah's address? I told her I was going to come by and help out for a bit."

"Yes, of course! It's 224 Acorn Lane. It's only two streets over from the elementary school; you can't miss it. And speaking of helping, I have a question to ask you when you get back."

"Yeah, no problem. I should be back in a few hours."

"Great! Have fun, dear."

Sarah lived in a brick townhouse on the corner of the street. The houses were clumped together into groups of four, and hers was on the end with a bright red door. The lights were on inside, but the curtains were drawn, so I couldn't see if anyone was inside as I walked up to the front door.

My heart skipped a beat as I raised my hand to ring the doorbell. Without a phone, I had no way of telling her that I planned on coming over, so I wasn't sure if she would be available. My mind raced through different scenarios of what she would say or do when she opened the door. Perhaps she had others over, or I was bothering her in the middle of something, or maybe she was on her way out, or, even scarier, maybe she would want me there and pull me into the house and kiss me wildly.

My heart stopped as I heard the red door unlock, and Sarah, dressed in a pair of gray sweatpants and a fluffy pink hoodie, opened the door. Her hair was pulled up into a frizzy bun of curls, but her face looked fresh and bright.

"Emily! Hey, come on in. Sorry I look like a mess," she said, hugging me and closing the door behind us, "I've been cleaning up around the house a bit today."

Her home was tiny and a bit cramped. Directly to the right was a narrow staircase, and down the hall, I could see what looked like a living room. There was a doorway on the left that had a bright light coming from it, which looked like it might be the kitchen. Her house smelled of warm candles and spiced meat.

"Come, sit down," she gestured me to a gray suede couch in the living room, taking a seat beside me, "How's John?"

"He is doing much better. Kiuchi has been taking care of him. They will be here for a few more days."

"Is she the young woman who was sitting next to him at Thanksgiving dinner?"

"Yeah, that's her."

"She seemed sweet. Too bad they have to leave soon," she said, pulling her legs up onto the couch and propping her chin on her hand.

Even in such casual clothes, curled up on the couch, Sarah expressed an air of grace. I wanted to reach out and touch her, but it still felt wrong.

"It smells good in here," I said, changing the subject.

"Oh, thanks for reminding me," she said, standing up and adjusting her clothes, "I have to go stir the meatballs. I'm making homemade meatball marinara in my slow cooker for dinner tonight."

"That sounds good."

There were no paintings on the walls in the living room, except for one small painting of some sunflowers that hung on the back wall over the dining table. There was also a small TV on a wooden stand with a gaming system hooked up and a single controller sitting on top. There was no coffee table. The whole place was surprisingly bare from what I had expected from a creative person like Sarah.

"Alright," she said, entering the room again, "It should be done in a few hours. Until then, are you ready for some decorating?"

"Yep, that's why I'm here," I said, standing from the couch. It was kind of a lie. I was there for her.

I was glad I'd kept my shoes on, because we started our work outside. Behind her house was a storage shed where we got out two plastic tubs of decorations and a tall metal step ladder.

"Can you hold the ladder while I put up the lights?" she said, opening up one of the tubs and pulling out a ball of tangled plastic icicle lights.

"Of course."

I helped her untangle the lights, which was actually easier than it looked, and I set up the ladder in front of her door. Because it was a two-story house, there was no gutter down low, so she worked at clipping the lights above the doorframe and stringing them over to the window by the door.

"I'm up here looking like a hot mess, and you look so sweet today," she said, smiling down at me.

"Keyword: hot," I answered.

She giggled as she finished attaching the last bit of wire and draping the rest down the doorframe to the outside plug by the door. As she descended the ladder from adjusting a few bulbs on top of the door, she wobbled a bit, and my hands went instinctively to her hips. I held her all the way down, and my arms almost wrapped around her when she reached the bottom. I quickly remembered that we were outside and people could see us, so I took my hands back and moved the ladder.

"Ready?" she asked, holding the plug.

"Ready."

She plugged in the lights, and even with the sun still up, they twinkled a bright blue. It was supposed to snow any day, and I was surprised it hadn't already. The lights made me even more excited for the snow. They would look beautiful against the blanket of white. I hadn't seen snow in years.

"Perfect," I sighed, and she came to stand beside me and look at them herself. She nodded.

Next, we went inside with the second bin and started putting up the mini plastic tree. It was only about two feet high, but because the living room was so bare, it was more than enough to bring the holiday spirit to the room.

At the bottom of the tub were some plastic red ornaments and some silver tinsel. And hidden beneath all that was a small porcelain angel in a green velvet dress with long blonde hair and white feathered wings. She had a plastic clip under her dress to clip her atop the tree. I picked her up carefully, pulling her from the box to admire her. Although there was a beauty about her, the grand look of her brought back memories of the Catholic cathedrals and it made me a bit uneasy.

"She was my mother's angel," Sarah explained, standing over my shoulder.

"Are your parents still alive?" I asked.

"Yes. Both of them. She gave it to me when I moved away."

There was a short silence as she took the angel and clipped her on the top of the tree, smoothing out the wrinkles in her dress. The angel's stare was ice-cold.

"Are you religious?" I finally asked, my eyes not leaving the angel.

Sarah sighed, "It's complicated. I believe in God, but I struggle with the idea. I've always been told that God hates people like me. People like us…" She took a breath and took my hand, "I don't believe God made me like this just to hate me. But not everyone would agree."

"I don't believe God hates you," I said, brushing my thumb across her hand.

"What about you? Are you religious?" she asked.

I shook my head, "No. I never felt close to God, or any church, for that matter. My parents tried, but I guess it didn't work. Maybe it's just something wrong with me."

Sarah pulled me close to her and wrapped her arms around my waist, "You are beautiful, Emily."

I was scared, but I laid my head on her shoulder. She was soft and warm, and the smell of her vanilla perfume mixed sweetly with the spiced aroma of her house. And for a moment, I felt safe. We stood there like that for a while before she pulled away and continued pulling out decorations.

We stretched a red silk tablecloth over the small round dining table, and set up a metal centerpiece with green sparkly pillar candles. We then hung her stocking up beside the TV since she didn't have a fireplace, and put some holiday cookie cutters and little knick-knacks like that here and there around the house. Finally, the boxes were empty except for one final item: the mistletoe.

She reached down and took it from the box.

"Where should we hang the final decoration?" she asked shyly.

I reached out taking it from her hand, and lifted my arm to hold it above us, "I think it belongs here."

She smiled, and with one quick motion, I stepped forward, reached my arm around her waist, and pulled her into me, kissing her creamy lips. She kissed me back, wrapping her arms around my neck, and I dropped the mistletoe beside us, wrapping my other arm around her.

My heart felt light like I might float away. I'd never kissed anyone like that before. In fact, I'd never been kissed like that before, not the way Sarah kissed me. But I was glad she did.

Chapter 17

The meatballs that Sarah made for dinner tasted even more delicious than they smelled. She served them on chipped white plates with stained silverware, but they tasted like they had come straight out of the kitchen of a five-star restaurant. The meat was soft and juicy, spiced with visible rosemary and sage, and dripping with a thick red marinara sauce.

She opened us a bottle of red wine, which I was hoping would ease my nerves. While the food was delicious, and the night was perfect, I still had a heavy heart. My secret sat on the tip of my tongue and begged to be spoken. I rehearsed it over and over in my head, trying to come up with the best way to start: *Sarah, I've been meaning to tell you…There is something I need to say, but it's difficult…Sarah, there is something from my past you should probably know…Sarah…I'm married.*

Over dinner, she bubbled about the season and the fun arts and crafts she had planned for her students for the holidays. In between topics she would ask me about my plans, to which I shrugged and asked her more about her own plans in order to keep my speaking to a minimal.

After she wiped the last bit of sauce from the corner of her mouth with a paper napkin, she leaped from the table with a twinkle in her eye, saying, "Oh! It's dark now. Let's go outside and see how the lights look at night."

I stood, taking her hand and walking to the front door where we put on our coats, padding out barefoot onto her front porch. The lights twinkled, and their cool white lights matched the frosty air. I looked over to Sarah, who was beaming as she admired the holiday décor. Her breath billowed out in puffy white clouds.

"Sarah," I started, feeling the tingling of my tongue as my secret tried to come out.

"Yes?" She turned to me with a smile, crossing her arms with a slight shiver.

"There is something I need to tell you before anything else happens," I said, a shiver passing over me, but it wasn't the cold.

"Shh," she hushed me, "I don't want to talk about sad things or the past. I just want to be right here, right now, okay?"

"Right here, right now," I repeated with a sigh.

There was a moment of silence between us, and I tried to quiet the fear in my mind. I looked over her curls, her soft lips, her sparkling eyes, and the delicate way the twinkling icicles illuminated her fair complexion. Suddenly, the wind picked up, bringing not only her warm vanilla scent but also a few fluffy snowdrops that floated and landed quietly in her hair.

"Snow," I gasped, "It's snowing."

She looked up, and so did I. The snow fell in silence, as even the wind died down to nothing. Puffy white balls of fluff landed on my nose and eyelashes, melting instantly. I stuck my tongue out, catching a few snowflakes as Sarah and I giggled.

"Emily?" she asked, her voice more serious again, "Will you stay the night with me?"

My breath caught in my throat.

"Um, Sarah, I'm not sure. I don't want to take things too fast," I stuttered. I was still wrapping my mind around the idea that I had kissed a woman. I had no idea how to actually be with a woman, though. I wouldn't know what to do. And I couldn't be with her officially until I told her the truth about myself.

"Oh, okay. I understand," she said,

She sounded disappointed, but I knew I had made the right choice. I needed some time to think.

"How about I make us some hot chocolate to warm up, and you can head home?" she asked.

"Alright," I said, relaxing a bit, "But only if it has the little marshmallows in it."

She laughed, "I don't have the little ones, but I can toss in a big one if you'd like."

"Deal."

The hot chocolate was thick and sugary, and she wasn't kidding about the giant marshmallow. It became mushy and soaked up a lot of the drink, but it still tasted yummy, much like a donut dipped in coffee.

After a shy kiss goodbye, I walked back to the B&B. My head was swimming with even more questions than before I had gone to see her. She liked me, and I liked her back. That was easy enough to understand. But she didn't want us to be public, which I supposed was okay since I wasn't in a good place to be in a serious relationship, anyway. And yet, I wanted to be.

I had never imagined myself with a woman. But there was just something irresistible about Sarah. She was beautiful and bright. But there was still a knot in my stomach. I felt guilty. The little voices in my head reminded me that I was married, that this wasn't my place. That I'd somehow failed as a wife by kissing her because I was a cheater. And the voices of the Church rang in my head about the evils of homosexuality.

And even worse than all of that, there was a part of me that thought maybe she was just a rebound. What had made me feel like I was flying just a few minutes earlier was now making me feel like I was falling down into some deep, dark hole all alone.

Chapter 18

Margaret was waiting in the living room, knitting something pink and fluffy when I came in. I took off my coat, hanging it up by the door before going in to sit beside her on the couch. She had a fire going in the fireplace.

"Ah, Emily," she said, putting down her knitting needles, "How was your visit?"

"It was fine. We decorated her place for the holidays."

"Sounds like fun," she smiled, "I do have something to ask you, dear."

"Sure. Anything."

"While John is laid up, I was wondering if you would be the one to help me around here? I know you are still looking for a job, and I'd pay you. It's just some paperwork and fix-it stuff. I know he taught you a few things. So, what do you say?"

I looked around the room at the homey furniture, and at the cardboard boxes in the corner with tinsel sticking out from the sides. I needed the money. I knew I couldn't live off of my saved up cash forever. And if I really wanted to start establishing myself in the area, I needed to get a job and start looking for a place to live.

"Of course, Margaret. I'd love to help out. Are there specific hours you need me to work?" I asked.

"Oh, no. I'll just give you a list of tasks each day. It's easy, don't you worry. You can start tomorrow. Go get some sleep, dear," she smiled warmly, "Thank you so much, Emily."

"Anytime, Margaret. Goodnight," I said, giving her a hug before heading upstairs.

The pink room was quiet and cozy, but the open window created a black void in the wall, and I couldn't shake the feeling I was being watched. I crossed the room, shutting the curtains before rushing under the blankets of the pitch-black room and closing my eyes. The night was full of nightmares.

I tried to start the morning on a high note, and decided to focus my energy on the work ahead. My work at the B&B started with checking the visiting family out, finalizing payments, and filing receipts from their stay while Margaret cleaned out their room. John and Kiuchi had an emotional goodbye, and after they had exchanged numbers and she had left, he spent the rest of the day up in his room.

The busy work helped to keep my mind off of the recent events, and since they were the kind of secretarial duties I was used to, the chores felt natural to me. There were only a few bits of manual labor I had to do around the property over the next few days. The snow continued to fall in heavy blankets, and so I had to go out and shovel the walkway daily. But even with the few added difficult chores, I was able to get into a sort of routine after only a couple of days on the job.

Everything started to feel like it was coming together. Later that week, John felt well enough to help Margaret and me unpack the Christmas boxes. Once most of the decorations were unpacked and put up, we all decorated the tree together by the fireplace. Margaret shared funny stories of John from when he was younger, and John blushed and tried to change the subject while his fingers worked at knots in the strands of Christmas lights.

It was all so lighthearted and fun, but it didn't last long. I went to the kitchen to get some eggnog from the fridge. I placed the carton on a wooden serving tray with three of Margaret's mismatched mugs beside it. As I passed through the foyer to bring the drinks back, the new house phone rang on the table beside the front door.

I placed the tray on the round table in the middle of the foyer and grabbed the phone, picking up the pen beside it so I could take some notes for the customer. Margaret peeked her head around the corner.

"Hello. This is the Maple Creek Bed and Breakfast. How may I help you?" I asked.

"Hello?" A familiar voice spoke on the other side, "I'm looking for Emily Jacobson. But she might be using the name Emily Heart. Is she staying there with you? I'd like to speak with her."

My stomach tightened into knots, and I felt dizzy and cold. The pen dropped to the floor as I caught myself on the table. It was Hector. He had found me.

"Um...I...she isn't..." I stuttered.

"Emily! Emily? Is that you? Talk to me!" His voice dropped deeper, and his tone became more authoritative.

I stood, gasping for air as a tear escaped my eye. I didn't know what to do. But Margaret swooped over, snatching the phone from my hand. I was still paralyzed in place.

"Hello? I'm sorry, sir. That was my niece, Shelby. She is interning here, and she isn't very good with her phone etiquette yet. How may I help you?" There was a pause, and I could hear him yelling something on the other side of the phone. "No, sir. There is no one by that name staying here. Thank you for calling, and Merry Christmas."

She hung up the phone with a click and then continued, "Go sit down, sweetie. We need to talk."

My whole body was shaking as he guided me to sit on the couch. "John, I need to speak with Emily. Go make us soup or something for lunch."

He nodded, jumping to his feet, and silently exiting the room.

I could feel my eyes welling up with tears, and my hands were shaking uncontrollably. Margaret seemed calm.

"I'm so sorry," I cried, "I should have told you everything about me. I'm not who you think I am. I left my husband, and I've been hiding here."

"Good," she said, folding her arms, "You are halfway done. Listen, Emily. You can't just run away from men like him."

"I know, it was stupid," I said, wiping my tears.

96

"No! It was exactly the right move. But what I mean is that you can't just walk away and expect them to go away. Men like him, men like my son-in-law, John's father, they will follow you. You have to do everything in your power to keep them away. You need paperwork. I know you are still trying to figure things out, but at least get a restraining order."

"A restraining order?" I asked. I'd heard of them, but I hadn't really thought about getting one.

There was a part of me that honestly believed that Hector still loved me and that he would never hurt me. I wanted to think he was just hurt and emotional, but that even if he were to find me, it wouldn't be to hurt me. That maybe he would change somehow.

"Emily," she said more sternly, taking my hand, "I've already lost a daughter; don't let me lose a friend, too."

My heart shattered with her words, and I remembered the story that John had told me about his mother and how he knew something was wrong, but they could never do anything about it. But now it was my turn to do something.

"Okay, I'll go get a restraining order tomorrow," I nodded.

Margaret threw her arms around me, "Thank you!"

A few minutes later, John returned with bowls of chicken soup for each of us. We ate, and soon, the laughter returned. The rest of the day was spent decking the halls with tinsel, candles, and jingle bells.

Chapter 19

I did as Margaret suggested and filled out the paperwork for a restraining order the next day. Beside the desk at the courthouse, there were also pamphlets on the divorce process. I took one, quietly slipping it into my purse while assuring my sinking heart that it was just for informative purposes. Once the paperwork was filled out, I was given a court date for a few days later.

I stopped at a small park during my walk back to the B&B. My head was spinning and I thought a little fresh air would do me some good. There were a few kids there with their parents. Their book-bags were strewn around the equipment, since they had only just gotten out of class. Walking around the perimeter of the park was also an elderly couple in matching red jogging suits and hats.

I sat on one of the empty benches and took a few deep breaths, watching the cloud billow out into the cold air. There was still about a foot of snow piled up around the bench, and I quietly counted the footprints in the snow from people, animals, and little birds. I looked up again at the people in the park, and noticed that there was now a woman sitting on the bench on the far side of the park now. It was Sarah.

I hadn't talked to her in days, and I immediately found myself standing from my bench and crossing the park over to where she sat. I had no control over my steps or the pull that I felt in my chest, like a rope that tied me to her. Now, instead of footprints, I was counting how many bouncing ringlets framed her face.

"Sarah, hey. How are you?" I asked, a lot less confidently than it sounded in my head.

"Oh my gosh! Hey, Emily. It's so nice to see you here. I hate that you don't have a phone. I wish we could talk more. What have you been up to?" She patted the seat beside her, and I sat down.

"Oh, you know. Just helping out around the B&B while John recovers. We just finished decorating for the holidays so that when the next couple of visitors come in about a week, it will be all ready for them."

"That sounds fun. I had a wonderful time decorating my place with you, Emily. I was actually wondering..." she started, scooching a little closer to me on the bench, "I was wondering if maybe you would like to come over for Christmas Eve?"

"I'd love that," I smiled, excited to have another date planned with her. "So, what brings you to the park?"

"Oh, I come here all the time after work to get a breather before going home. It's really close to the school and my house, which is nice. What about you? What are you up to today?" she asked.

"I was, um...I was at the courthouse doing some paperwork," I said. I wanted so much, to be honest, but I also was afraid to tell her about Hector. I thought that if I told her, she might not want to see me anymore.

"Ugh. Moving, right? I hate having to go up and change my addresses and fill out paperwork for this and that."

"Um, yeah. It was paperwork. It wasn't fun," I said, fidgeting in my seat a bit.

Sarah and I weren't serious. At least, not yet. And disclosing information about exes, which is what I considered him, wasn't something I should disclose until the relationship got serious. Or at least, that's what I kept telling myself.

"Well, I've got to get home and grade these papers on writing ABCs. But it was great talking to you. I'm so glad we ran into each other. I hope we see each other more often."

With a quick hug, she swung her flower-covered tote bag of paperwork over her shoulder and walked away down the street. After a few more minutes of people-watching, I stood to go back to the B&B, but my foot snagged on something. I looked down to see that it was a lunchbox. It was purple with some elegant white flowers painted on the side. The artistic style made me think that it must have been Sarah's and that she had left it there by accident. So, I scooped it up and took it back with me.

I didn't take it to her house, though. The thought of her asking me to stay the night again worried me. Instead, the next morning, I made a little extra time after breakfast, and I took it over to the school to leave it in the office for her.

The inside of the school was painted with thick cream-colored paint, and there were little handmade paper crafts hung up and down the halls and on the door windows of gingerbread men, paper trees, and handprints from the students. Just inside the glass doors, on the right, was a dark green metal door with a silver sign with the word "office" etched into it.

 I turned the loose knob, and the door screeched open to reveal two women behind a tall desk who were surrounded by piles of paper and a couple of very outdated computers.

"May I help you?" asked the woman closest to me in a not-so-friendly voice.

She was a round woman in a purple cardigan over a black shirt. Her glasses, which were practically hanging off the end of her pointed nose, were the same color as her cardigan. And her short bob, which was cut and styled much like mine, framed her face in a way which only made it appear even rounder, and made me question if I should maybe grow my hair out a bit. The other woman remained silent.

"Um, yes. I hope so. I'm looking for Sarah Norman?" I asked, looking at both of them.

"And what would you like with her?" the woman in purple asked.

"She forgot her lunchbox at the park. I was just bringing it back to her," I answered, lifting it to show her.

"I think she just went into the copy room back here; let me go check for you," smiled the other woman.

She was dark-skinned with long black hair, and she spoke with an accent that I couldn't put my finger on, but her tone was much friendlier. She swooped out of the room in a red knit dress with a pair of fuzzy-looking black leggings and matching boots. The first woman just continued to glare at me over her glasses.

"Here she comes," the second woman said, coming back into the room and taking her seat.

A moment later, Sarah came out and walked up to the counter beside the woman in purple.

"Hey! Thanks for bringing this to me," she said. She was bright as always, but there was something different in the way she looked at me.

"Yeah, no problem. I cleaned it out for you, too, and I made you a sandwich, just in case," I smiled, handing her the lunchbox over the counter.

"Oh, you didn't have to do that," she answered in an odd tone.

"Do you know her?" the woman in purple asked, turning over her shoulder to look at Sarah with a raised eyebrow.

"Yes, this is Emily Heart," Sarah explained, "She is one of my art students. Well, thanks again." Sarah scurried from the room before I could get another word in, and the woman in purple returned her harsh gaze to me as if inviting me to leave. And so I did.

I couldn't shake the feeling that there was something a bit off about my encounter with Sarah. A part of me felt rejected in some sort of abstract way. I mean, I didn't expect her to come flying over the counter to kiss me or anything, but she basically made me sound like I was just someone she barely knew.

Maybe it's because I didn't stay the night. Maybe she felt like I didn't want to date her... I thought. So, since she invited me over for Christmas Eve, I decided that I would try to do something to make it special and hopefully tell her how I really felt. But first, I needed the perfect gift.

Chapter 20

The hearing for my restraining order went well. At least, as good as something like that can go. Part of me felt like I was betraying Hector. But when they read the messages he had left me on my social media page out loud, a shiver of fear ran down my spine again, and I was relieved at the thought of having legal protection against him, just in case he really did want to hurt me.

One of the security guards by the door stopped me on my way out. She was a middle aged woman with a blonde ponytail and dark circles under her eyes. She looked frail, but her eyes were sharp.

"Excuse me," she said in the kind of voice that makes you stop what you are doing and pay attention, "I don't mean to pry, but I heard part of your hearing saying that you are getting a restraining order on your husband?"

Hearing that sentence made me feel like I had swallowed a rock. A really big rock. I tried to paint on a confident face as best as I could.

"Yes, that is correct," I answered, my nose in the air.

"Well, I don't mean to give you unsolicited advice, but is that really the kind of man you want to call your husband? If I were you, I wouldn't be filing for just a restraining order. I'd be filing for divorce."

I knew she was right. It was the reason I picked up the pamphlet earlier that week, and it was the reason why I didn't have any plans set for moving back to California. The word divorce, for whatever reason, was just difficult to comprehend. I didn't go into my marriage planning for a divorce. It just felt so final, so ominous. It felt like I had failed somehow.

"I know it seems bad, but you are still young. You have a long life ahead of you, and you can make it one filled with love. Marriage is just a paper, and so is a divorce. What matters is spending time with the ones who love you and those who treat you right."

I thought of Margaret and John and their kindness in inviting me into their lives. And I thought of Sarah, and the warm glow she gave off, and the way I felt lighter when I was around her. Then, I looked down at my empty left hand and saw how easy it was to take off his ring when I left. I knew I never wanted to put it back on. I never wanted to feel the way he made me feel again.

I nodded to the woman in agreement, and she smiled back at me, pointing down the hall.

"There is a lawyer just down the hall that can help you. He is a divorce lawyer. He can give you the paperwork you will need. God bless you, and have a happy holiday," she said, going back to work.

I walked down the hall to an office with a fancy metal sign that read 'Tyler Martin, Divorce Lawyer.' Beneath the shiny placard was a torn piece of paper that was hanging loosely from the door by a small strip of tape. The paper had a note scribbled on it, which read 'Out to Lunch. I'll be back at 1.'

With a sigh, I decided to come back later, and instead, I walked down to old Main Street, where there were a few small shops filled with boutique-style clothes, handmade soaps, and antique jewelry. I knew I needed to get the perfect gift for Sarah and I's Christmas Eve together. This time, I knew I was going to do it: I was going to tell Sarah how I felt about her. And I was even going to tell her who I really was and that I was getting a divorce.

I had never really shopped for another girl, at least not for the kind of present I was looking for. I started in the clothing shops and browsed through racks of blouses and sweaters, but I decided against buying any of them. Clothes made strange Christmas gifts, and I didn't know her size or style.

Next, I went to the handmade soap shop. It was bright, full of pastel colors, and it smelled like the perfume section at the mall. The walls were lined with clear bowls and painted wood crates filled with every type of soap imaginable. They had bars of hand and body soaps, liquid soaps, shampoos, laundry soaps, dish soaps, and even soap for pets. While it was all beautiful and smelled delightful, I was internally cringing at the implication of giving someone soap and was already thinking of a million different ways she could take it wrong when something caught my eye.

By the door was a pyramid tower of round soaps about the size of baseballs. They were mint green and labeled 'Mistletoe Kiss Bath Bombs.' The thought of Sarah and I's mistletoe kiss crossed my mind, causing me to lick my lips. The thought of taking a bath with her caused my heart to flutter as I picked up a bath bomb and rushed it to the register for checkout.

The cashier wrapped it in red tissue paper and laid it gently in a holiday themed paper bag, decorated with green peppermint stripes. I took it, walking out of the store feeling giddy that I had found something for Sarah. But it wasn't enough.

The gift was cute. Sweet, even. But it wasn't serious or heartfelt. As I passed one of the antique shops in search of a more meaningful gift to accompany the bath bomb, I saw a sign in the window for 50% off jewelry, and I decided to take a look. The store was all dark and dusty with crowded aisles of knick-knacks and old furniture. Dim yellowed lamps lit the rooms with an eerie glow.

In the center of the large main room, beside the cash registers, were glass cases filled with various styles of antique jewelry. There were golden broaches, matching necklaces, and earring sets covered in gaudy green and blue clusters of jewels and rings the size of golf balls in intricate designs. None of them seemed to say, 'I really like you.' So, I left and headed back to the Bed and Breakfast.

Chapter 21

When I arrived back at the B&B, John was sipping a cup of tea in the living room. He seemed relaxed as he stared into the crackling fireplace. His face was still bruised a bit, but he was already looking so much better.

"Hello, John. How are you?" I asked, peeking my head in.

"Hey, Emily. I'm doing well today; I've just been taking a breather. Would you like to come sit with me for a moment?"

"Sure," I said, taking a seat beside him on the couch and placing my green shopping bag on the coffee table.

"Grams told me you went in today for the hearing on your restraining order. I just wanted to make sure you are doing okay. Did it go well?"

"It did, actually. They still have to serve it to him, but I'm already feeling a bit better just knowing I have one now."

"Good, good. I'm glad. And what is this fun little bag?" he asked, pointing to the green soap bag.

"Oh, that's just a Christmas gift for Sarah," I shrugged.

"Sarah?" he asked, with a scheming sort of grin on his face. "Well, I actually have something I'd like for you to give her for me."

"Oh?" I asked, a bit confused as to why he couldn't simply give it to her himself since they were so close.

"Come with me," he said, taking my hand and leading me up the stairs, practically skipping a step or two as he did.

He took me into his room, leaving the door open and releasing my hand to pull something out from under the bed. He placed a nice-looking green jewelry box down on the bed and opened up the gold clasp, reaching in to pull out a small necklace.

He turned to me, holding it by the chain to let the charm on the end dangle in the light. It was a small golden heart-shaped locket.

"It's beautiful," I whispered.

"It was one of my mother's," he said, "She bought it for herself for her birthday one year. My father wasn't much of a gift giver, so she would sometimes buy herself little things instead."

"You want to give this to Sarah?" I asked.

He placed the locket in my hand, "No, I want you to give it to Sarah. Sarah is a close friend of mine, and I think she deserves someone who can see how wonderful she is. She deserves someone like you. I can see the way you look at her."

I shook my head, "No. John, this locket is too special. This is yours."

"It just brings back bad memories, and it wasn't bought in love. I was hoping, maybe, you could give it new memories. Give it love."

I couldn't help but hug him. He really was an angel to me.

"Now," he said, stepping away, "My head is hurting a bit. Would you mind finishing up some of the phone calls for the reservations for next week so I can take a nap?"

"Not at all. Sleep well, John. Thank you. Really. This is so special."

I took the locket down the hall to my room and sat on the edge of the bed, turning the locket over in my palm. It was only about the size of a dime, and the inside, where the pictures usually were, was blank. The outside was shiny, and there were almost no scratches or blemishes at all on the heart, save for a few small marks by the clasp.

I held the locket to my heart. Even though it was small, it held a lot of weight, and I needed to find a way to lighten it. I needed a way to make it my own and give it a new purpose. And then it hit me: I could have it engraved.

After placing it in one of the drawers of my dresser, I went down stairs to finish the work that needed to be done around the B&B while John rested and Margaret prepared dinner. And once I was finished, I wrapped my red coat around myself, the necklace tucked inside my pocket, and snuck out the front door and back down the sidewalk towards old Main Street.

There, in a brick building on the corner, was a small jewelry shop that did repairs, sizing, and various other jewelry services. I took the locket inside and up to a glass counter where an elderly man was sitting. He had frizzy white hair and thick glasses that made him look a bit like a bug, and he was reading a book on birdwatching.

"Hello," I smiled, removing the necklace from my pocket and placing it on the counter between us.

The man put down his book, looked down at the necklace, and then silently back at me.

"I was wondering," I continued, "if I could get this engraved?"

"Hmm," he grunted, leaning forward and picking up the necklace, looking at it from all angles. "When?"

"By Christmas Eve," I said tentatively. I had never had anything engraved, and so I was unaware of how long it usually took.

"What do you want engraved on it?" he asked. His voice was scratchy and gruff.

"On the inside, I was hoping to get Sarah on one side and Emily on the other."

"A sister gift, then?" he grumbled under his breath, "Yes, well, it will be very small letters."

"That's perfect. I don't want to alter the necklace too much, and I'm not looking for anything flashy."

"I can have it ready the day before Christmas Eve. But be sure to pick it up then, because I'll be closed for the holidays. Don't want your sister going without a Christmas present," he said, pulling out a piece of layered paper and filling it out with a shaking hand before tearing off the top and handing me the pink piece underneath.

"Oh, she isn't my sister," I said, taking the paper and turning to leave.

"Oh?"

"She's," I started, my voice trailing off. *What would Sarah be? I haven't asked her out yet...*I thought. "Never mind. Well, thank you. Have a nice day."

"Mhm," he waved, taking the necklace and disappearing behind a curtain in the back corner of the shop.

Chapter 22

Time passed quickly, and before I knew it, it was Christmas Eve. I'd been unable to catch a time that the divorce lawyer was open, and since his office was closed for the holidays, I decided to put off the divorce until after New Year's. We had two new sets of guests, but neither of them spent much time at the B&B, and they spent most of their time out and about, visiting relatives.

I had picked up the glistening necklace the night before, and it was absolutely perfect. Our names were written in thin, sweeping letters, and he even cleaned the locket for me at no extra charge. I had nothing to wrap it in, so instead, I wore it under my turtleneck, out of sight.

I'd chosen a red turtleneck, black slacks, and a pair of black strappy heels to wear for the night. While my short blonde hair couldn't be pulled back, I did clip my bangs back into a 90s bump in an attempt to look sophisticated or something like that. I slipped on my coat and boots, and with the green soap bag in hand, I made my way to Sarah's house in the snow. I was confident and felt like I could handle anything the night had to offer, or at least, that's what I thought.

I knocked on Sarah's door, and it swung open within seconds. Sarah stood in the doorway, her arms crossed and her eyebrows buttoned together as she looked me up and down. She was dressed in a pair of gray sweatpants and a plain black hoodie, and her hair was in a messy bun. Her eyes were red and puffy, like she had been crying.

"Sarah? Are you okay?" I asked. When I took a step towards her, she took a step back.

"What is wrong with you? I mean, seriously. You think after what you did, you can just come over here, all dressed up like nothing's wrong?" Her voice was sharp and accusatory.

"What? What did I do? I don't understand."

"Oh, of course. Play dumb. I mean, I know we aren't going out or anything, but at least now I know why. You were just messing around with me. Well, fine. Hope you had fun," she snapped, starting to close the door.

My hand shot out, stopping the door as I pleaded, "Sarah, I mean it. I really don't understand what you are talking about. Please, tell me. Let's talk."

She paused then opened the door again, standing to the side to let me in before closing the door behind us. And for a moment we stood in silence before she re-crossed her arms and explained, looking down at the floor.

"I tried to find you on social media to send you a friend request. And I found you, but you were posing in pictures with some man you never mentioned. You never told me you were married."

"Oh my God! Sarah, I'm so sorry. I meant to tell you, but I was scared. I was going to tell you tonight. It's true, I'm married. But not for long. I'm working on

114

a divorce right now," I said, dropping the gift bag by the door and taking her hand.

She still wouldn't look at me as she continued, "Oh, yeah. Sure. One of those types that is always saying you are going to leave them, but you never do, and then I'm going to become your girl on the side."

"I'd never do something like that, Sarah. You aren't my girl on the side. I really am leaving my husband. That's why I'm here in Maple Creek. I'm taking a breather and looking into getting a job and a place out here. I left California for good."

"Really?" she asked, looking up at me with tear-stained cheeks.

"Yes, really. In fact," I said, taking my hand back and reaching up to undo the necklace, "I didn't just come here for our date. I came here to ask you something."

"What's this?" she asked as I laid the locket in her hand.

"I know you aren't much for PDA, and I know that I am working on a lot of things in my life right now, but I wanted to tell you that you are beautiful. I have been so used to being oppressed and not allowed to speak my mind since meeting my soon-to-be ex-husband. But since I met you, I have become stronger and bolder, and I want to start following my heart instead of being told what is right for me. And my heart wants you. Sarah, will you be my girlfriend?"

Her tears started flowing again as she threw her arms around me, clasping the locket in her hand, and I held her there for a while until her sobbing stopped. I took the locket from her hand, put it on her, and hugged her again.

"Oh, no! I didn't end up making any dinner," she said, stepping back and wiping her tears on her sleeve.

"I was here for you, not the food," I smiled, "How about I order some pizza?"

She squealed, "I'd love that! But I need to make something. It's Christmas Eve. You can use my phone to order. It's on the coffee table." Sarah ran to her fridge and swung open the door, her eyes darting around, looking for something to make.

I took off my jacket and hung it by the door, then picked up her phone and looked for the number of the pizza place. "What type of pizza would you like?"

"Cookies!" she yelled happily.

"What?"

"I'll make cookies tonight. I still have a roll of sugar cookie dough."

"Oh," I laughed, probably harder than I should have.

"What? You don't like sugar cookies?" she asked, coming back to stand in front of me, dough in hand.

"Of course I do," I smiled, waving the phone at her, "But I had asked what kind of pizza you wanted."

She looked at the phone and then back to me, giggling, "Oh! That's funny. No, not a cookie pizza. Actually, I like meat lovers with extra bacon."

"Sounds perfect to me."

Sarah threw a dozen cookies in the oven, and they were finished just as the delivery man showed up with our large pizza. I tipped him a bit extra because of the snow and the fact that he wasn't wearing a heavy enough jacket for the weather. Plus, it was Christmas Eve.

Sarah turned on the game console and put in a DVD that turned the TV screen into a looped video of a crackling fire. Even though the fire was digital, it added a sense of warmth to the room. We were both curled up on the couch, and neither of us really touched our pizza. Instead, we delved into deeper questions about each other, sort of like a session of the Twenty Questions game.

I found myself asking more and more questions as we went along, because, although I had been so drawn to her, I realized that I knew very little about her. And as our questions game went on, I was happy to find that I liked her even more with every answer.

Sarah was 27, she loved cats, and was an only child. She liked modern art, cake decorating, and used to have a stamp collection until she lost it during her last move. She had never really dated any other women before me, but had known she liked girls since she was 14.

She had an almost sorta kinda girlfriend in high school. They were both cheerleaders, and they would often kiss behind the bleachers late at night after the games. But when Sarah tried to go public about their relationship, the other girl laughed in her face and told everyone she was crazy and that she was just obsessed with her. After that, and after she had heard her father rant about "fags" when a news article came out

117

advertising a local Pride parade, she decided to focus on work and school instead.

But then, she said, when I came to town, she could tell I had been through pains of my own and that, just maybe, I could help her heal past hers. She said that she could see that I was strong, and she had felt drawn to me because of it. I took her hand and placed it in my lap, wrapping it up in both of my hands.

I didn't feel strong. I still had no idea where I was going to work or live, and the idea of filing those divorce papers gave me a stomach ache. I was terrified. But I could tell by the look in her eyes that she meant what she said. And I thought, at least in those few moments, that maybe I could be strong.

When it was my turn, I told her how much I loved classic novels and cozy mysteries, and that I listened to rap, but on rainy days I liked to listen to smooth jazz. I told her about growing up in Maple Creek, and about California, and about Hector. I skipped the part about my parent's death, because I wanted to keep the mood up.

After our conversations, there was one thing that we definitely agreed on: the sugar cookies tasted best when we kissed them off each other's lips.

Chapter 23

"So what's in the bag?" she asked, bringing it into the living room after putting our dishes in the kitchen.

"Oh! I completely forgot about it. That's just another little gift I got you."

"Another gift? Can I open it?"

"Yes, of course."

Her dainty fingers rustled through the tissue paper, carefully unwrapping the ball of soap. She held it to the light.

"It's a bath bomb," I explained, "It made me think of you."

"Mistletoe kiss?" she asked. "It's perfect! Would you like to try it with me?"

"With you?" I asked, my hands getting sweaty at the thought.

"Mhm," she smiled, "But before we do that, I need to give you your gift."

Sarah pulled a thin green folder out of her black duffle art bag by the front door and thumbed through the papers inside. She then pulled a single sheet from the back of the folder and handed it to me. The page looked like some sort of flier. It read:

Valentine's Art Show
Debut Artists:
Lin Zhu
Nicholas Lowery
Emily Heart

"Debut artist?" I smiled, "What is this for?"

"A few times a year, I coordinate a gallery exhibition at the downtown library. It's nothing too fancy, but it's a lot of fun. People in the town enter for a chance to get their art hung up there, but I get to choose a few spotlight artists if my students show particular talent. I chose you to have a spot for your work at the upcoming show," she explained, tucking a stray curl behind her ear.

"I've never been in a real art show before. This is so exciting! Thank you so much," I said, hugging her and looking back over the paper.

"Now," she said, holding up the bath bomb, "How about a nice hot bath?"

My stomach fluttered, and I bit my lip, "Um, yeah. Sure. I've never tried a bath bomb before. Sounds fun."

"Come on," she squealed, taking my hand and pulling me from the couch.

We dashed up the stairs, giggling like schoolgirls as we reached the bathroom. It was decorated simply, like the rest of her house. There was a silver soap dispenser on the sink beside a fake plant in a clear vase. There were some white towels folded on a rack over the toilet, and the shower only contained a bar of soap, a bottle of two-in-one hair wash, and a pink razor. The shower curtain that she pushed aside was a plain light blue cloth.

Sarah turned on the water, put the plug in the tub, placed the bath bomb on the sink, and started to undress. Her black hoodie brushed up her body and off her shoulders, and she dropped it to the floor beside her. Then, she hooked her thumbs into the elastic band on her sweatpants, and they slipped gracefully down her hips and joined her hoodie on the floor.

Her skin was like soft ivory against the black lace of her panties and matching bra. The lace trim perfectly framed her lovely, lush breasts and firm cheeks. Her stomach was soft. It wasn't flat, but her curves were smooth like the strokes of a paintbrush.

She leaned over, running her hand under the faucet, and I couldn't help but keep my eyes from wandering some more up and down her legs and her back. She was like a work of art. And, to my surprise, I became immediately aroused, my own panties becoming increasingly wet and warm. My thighs began to tingle. "Oh, sorry," she said, bumping into me as she stepped back, "I just got so excited, and here I am, throwing my clothes off like a whore." A blush flushed over her face and chest.

"Don't be sorry," I assured her, "I'm excited, too."

I reached down to pull up my turtleneck, but my hands froze. I was suddenly very self-conscious. I didn't have Sarah's curves. I was flat-chested and kind of bony, with a bit of a tummy on me. And I wasn't as neat with my bikini line as she was. I was mentally beating myself up over not taking a more delicate time to prepare for our date.

"May I help?" Sarah asked, reaching down and unbuttoning my slacks.

I smiled awkwardly, and my heart was beating itself against my chest so forcefully that I was afraid she might hear it. But I continued with the motion I had started. With shaking hands, I lifted my shirt over my head, dropping it to the ground beside me to join her clothes. And my pants followed.

My bra and panties were both cotton, and not matching in color, or pattern. I gazed down at the floor, too afraid to meet eyes with Sarah and see her reaction. Suddenly, her fingers were under my chin, and she lifted my head, and planted a soft kiss on my lips.

"Beautiful," she whispered.

Sarah then reached over to turn off the water and unwrapped the plastic from the bath bomb, "Ready?"

"Ready," I said, feeling more relaxed.

She leaned over and dropped the bath bomb into the water, and it immediately began to fizz and fill the tub with a bright green foamy color and little bits of red glitter. The bathroom was filled with the scent of cranberries and sugar.

"Wow, so cool!" Sarah giggled.

Then, she turned back to me with a more serious expression. I took a deep breath. I knew what came next: I had to get completely naked. Sarah took my hands and placed them behind her, on her bra clasp.

"Are you sure you are okay with this?" she asked, looking deep into my eyes.

I was nervous, but I definitely wanted to continue, "Yes."

My fingers fumbled with the clasp until it popped open, and she slid the straps down her shoulders. Her breasts were perfect and round. I wanted to touch them. I ran my fingertips across her back and up over the side of her breasts. As I did, she reached behind me and undid my bra as well, caressing my nipples gently with her thumbs.

We both dropped our panties, and she stepped into the bathtub, offering me her hand to help me in. The water was actually really hot, but the foamy bubbles felt amazing on my skin. We sat facing each other, caressing one another's legs and arms and exploring one another with our fingertips in the sloshing silence of her bathroom.

That was until I started to cry. It happened out of nowhere. One moment, I felt bliss and the next...dread. Memories of what he had done to me came flooding back, and so did all my pain.

"Emily! Emily, are you okay?" Sarah wrapped her arms around me as I sobbed.

The crying led to soft sobs, which led to more sweetly soft kisses and the kisses eventually led to me cuddling in her lap with my back against her bare chest. Her legs were on either side of me, and I laid my head back against her shoulder. The water was at the edge of the tub, and I kept especially still to keep it from spilling over.

"Are you...I mean, are you okay?" she asked, her voice shaking.

"Yes. I think so. It's not you. It's just...it's...the last time I was naked with someone wasn't...romantic."

A silence passed between us for a few moments. Her hands were wrapped around me, and I felt so calm and so secure that I thought I might fall asleep right there in the tub with her.

"And with me?" she asked.

"With you, it's...different. Different good. I really like you, Sarah."

She kissed the top of my head and ran her fingers through my dampened hair.

"So," Sarah finally spoke again, "I know it is really early to ask this, so feel free to say no, but tomorrow, my parents are coming over to visit me for Christmas. I know you are busy at the B&B, but do you think you could stop by tomorrow? I'd like for you to meet them."

I thought back to the last girl she tried to be more public with and the way she had been humiliated. I didn't want to do that to her, too. And I was trying to take my relationship with her more seriously. *I'm getting a divorce, and soon I won't be married...*I reminded myself.

"Yes, I'd love to meet your parents," I nodded, sloshing the water out of the tub as I turned to look at her.

"Thank you," she said kissing me sweetly, "I'm so excited for Christmas, now."

Her hands reached between my legs, caressing the inside of my thighs. At first, it felt nice, making a warm tingle run down my spine. But as she made her way up to my pussy, my breath caught, I tightened up and flinched away from her. I didn't mean to; it just happened. The forceful touch of my ex rushed into my mind, and I began to tear up. She pulled her hand away slowly and reached up to pet my hair, kissing my shoulder.

"It's okay," she whispered, "Let's go downstairs."

After our bath, we both dressed and ate some more pizza because we were actually hungry then, and I went back to the B&B. I could barely sleep that night. For the first time since I was little, I, too, was excited for Christmas Day.

Chapter 24

Christmas morning at the B&B was bright and festive. The breakfast table was filled with new guests, so John and I took some food to the living room to munch on. One of the visiting families, a mother, a father, and twin teenage boys, were all dressed up in their Sunday best, including suits and ties, and the mother wore a red holiday dress. The other guests, an elderly couple and their special needs daughter, were happily dressed in comedically ugly sweaters of bright green with real light-up lights woven into them.

Aside from a few pleasantries, the guests each kept to their own group over breakfast. Once they had all left to go see their families in town, Margaret and I cleaned up, which went a lot faster than I had expected, even with the mountains of dishes. Perhaps it was my festive cheer that made the chores go faster. After everything was back in order again, Margaret, John, and I convened in the living room for presents.

For John and Margaret, I had made them each hand-painted Christmas cards earlier in the month: a gingerbread man for Margaret, and a snowman for John. Each of the cards had a hand-written message in it, thanking them for their hospitality.

John gave Margaret a new cooking apron that was decorated with daisies, which made me smile at the thought that he probably got her the sunflower one she was always wearing. For me, John had bought a warm red hat with a gigantic puffy fluff ball on top that was nearly the size of a grapefruit. It made me laugh.

Margaret gave John some paperwork that said she had paid to upgrade his phone plan to allow international calls so that he could call Kiuchi more often. It brought a tear to John's eye, and he hugged her tightly. Then, Margaret handed me a packet of paper with a red bow stuck to the top corner. It read 'Job Application.'

"I'm getting older, you know," she said, leaning forward and whispering like she was telling me a secret, "You have been such a wonderful help to me and John. I'd like for you to keep on working here. You will be an official employee with a real salary."

"Oh my goodness! Thank you so much. I'd love to work here," I exclaimed, throwing my arms around them both.

"Merry Christmas, everyone," Margaret said with a small sigh.

Soon after the presents, Margaret started the fire in the living room fireplace and sat down with her knitting. John sat in the dining room and started texting. I assumed he was Kiuchi, based on his blushing and smile.

I went upstairs and got cleaned up into some slacks and a cream sweater. I put on a dash of makeup, then bundled up to head over to Sarah's house for Christmas afternoon. I was both terrified and excited to meet her parents.

When I arrived, there was a shiny black truck parked out on the street in front of her house. Sarah opened the door for me excitedly within moments of me knocking on her door. Her usually quiet haven wasn't quiet anymore, though. There were pops and crackles coming from the kitchen and a low, rumbling voice coming from the living room.

"Is that Emily?" shouted her father from the couch.

"Yes, Daddy," she answered, helping me with my coat.

"Oh! Emily, how nice to meet you," Sarah's mother shouted from the kitchen.

Everyone seemed much happier than I had expected. There wasn't any twinge of sarcasm in their voices at all. At least, not that I could tell.

"Everything going okay?" I whispered to Sarah.

"Yeah, of course," she said with a smile. But it wasn't an intimate smile like the night before. She looked at me the same way she did when I took her lunch to her at the school a few weeks before. I could feel my heart sink. I had a feeling there was something she wasn't telling me.

I hung up my coat and new hat by the door, and Sarah took me into the kitchen, where her mom was cooking some sort of stir-fried vegetable dish. Her mother looked kind of like a librarian. She had thick glasses that covered almost all of her face, and her gray hair was pulled back into a tight bun. She was wearing a dark green cardigan over a white turtleneck and black slacks, and the way she wore the outfit really outlined her pear-shaped figure.

"I'm so glad you were able to join us for Christmas, Emily," she said without looking up from the food she was cooking.

"Thank you. I'm glad to be here with Sarah," I said a little hesitantly.

"Do you need any help, mom?" Sarah asked, dipping her finger into a plastic bowl with what looked like some sort of cake batter in it and licking it off of her fingers.

"Yeah," her mother said, "I need you to get out of the kitchen and stop sticking your fingers in the food."

Sarah giggled and walked out of the kitchen, gesturing for me to follow her into the living room.

"Hey, whatcha doing?" Sarah asked her father, taking a seat beside him on the couch.

"Just staring at this dumb fire," he grumbled, pointing to her TV, "I can't believe you don't have cable."

"I have some video games if you want to try that," she said, starting to get up from her seat.

"What am I? 12?" he huffed.

Her father looked older than I had imagined he would. His hair was thinning, but he still appeared to trim it into an almost military-style haircut. He wore a green plaid shirt and a pair of jeans, and his face was frozen in a grimace.

"Sorry," he said, softening a bit and turning to me, "I'm just really hungry. I hate waiting for food. It's nice to meet you, Emily. I'm glad Sarah finally has a friend."

"A friend?" I asked, and I looked at Sarah.

Sarah's eyes were pleading, and my eyes darted down the chain around her neck. She was wearing a green v-neck sweater that allowed the pendant to rest perfectly on her chest. Except, it wasn't her locket that was on the end of the chain. Instead, it was a silver crucifix. My chest felt tight all of a sudden.

"I see," I continued, "Well, I'm glad I could stop by, but unfortunately I can't stay. It was nice to meet you."

I walked straight to the front door and grabbed my coat and hat off of the hook, throwing them on as I walked out the door. As I closed the door, Sarah caught it and stepped outside with me and closed the door behind us. She was barefoot, and she wrapped her arms around herself to keep warm.

"You didn't tell them?" I asked, "I thought you invited me to Christmas with your family so that we could tell them. I know we aren't public, but why did you want me to meet your parents if I'm just going to be your friend to them?"

"I'm scared," she admitted, "I've never told them that I'm a lesbian. And they are going to hate me. You don't understand."

"Yes, I do! My parents were also strict, but I stood up to them years ago," I snapped.

"Standing up and leaving aren't the same thing. I want my parents in my life. I love them."

Something about what she said felt like a dagger in my chest. But I knew she was right. I never wanted my parents to stay in my life after I left. I didn't love them, at least not like that.

I took a deep breath, and looked at my beautiful girlfriend who was freezing on the front step, and at her necklace. She reminded me of myself when I still lived with parents.

"You don't have to tell them if you don't want to. I understand," I reassured her. "But, if you want to, I'm here for you. No matter what they say, I'll be here." She nodded slowly, "Will you stay for Christmas?" "Come here," I said, wrapping my arms around her as she shivered, "Of course. I'm so sorry, Sarah. I was just caught off guard. I don't like having to switch between being close and being distant all the time."

"Maybe I can find a way to tell them. Just not today. I'm not ready," she whispered.

I played my fingers in her curls and she pulled away and looked at me with sweet eyes. She got up on her tiptoes and gave me a kiss on my forehead. But just as she did, the front door swung open. It was her mother.

"Sarah, I'm going to need you in the kitchen in a few minutes to help me with…" she stopped and looked between us, "Oh. I see."

Sarah's mouth was agape, and her eyes were wide. Her mother's mouth, on the other hand, was pursed shut. After a few more frozen, silent moments, she spoke again.

"I need to see you in the house now, Sarah. I'm sure your father will want to talk to you about this. Goodbye, Emily."

"No," I said, taking her hand, "I'm staying with Sarah."

Her mother glared at me, but after a pause, she said, "Fine."

Sarah looked at me, tears now streaming quietly down her face, and she was shivering even harder. I squeezed her hand and gave her a nod, and she and I went back into the house to face her parents.

Chapter 25

Sarah's mother went immediately over to her father and whispered in his ear, then turned to us with one more sharp look, and went quietly back into the kitchen.

"Sarah! In here. Now," her father barked.

She shook off my hand and went to stand in the living room; her eyes were turned down. I stood beside her, watching her face.

"So, you and this woman here are pretending to be some sort of couple? Did it ever occur to you that you two are both women? You are a disgusting sinner. What do you have to say for yourself?"

"Daddy, please, just listen," she begged, almost hysterically.

"No! You listen. You are my daughter, and I will not have you living like this. I didn't raise you like this," he snapped. His face was turning purple, and his hands were shaking, but he stayed seated.

Sarah broke down in tears, and I wrapped her in my arms, letting her cry on my shoulder. "It's going to be okay," I whispered.

"You are going to rot in Hell, and I'm not having you drag me down with you. You are no longer my daughter. If you want to live like this, that's fine.

But you aren't any part of my life. Come on, Carol! We are leaving."

Sarah's mother stepped silently out of the kitchen, putting on a black all-weather coat, and Sarah's father threw on a big brown leather coat. Then, the two of them walked out the door without looking back.

Sarah collapsed to the floor, sobbing uncontrollably, and I sat beside her and rubbed her back in the silence. After a while, her sobs became quiet tears, and she lay on the couch.

I went into the kitchen and made sure everything was turned off, and I cleaned up a bit, wrapping up the cooked food, throwing out the rest, and washing the dishes for Sarah. I then went back to the living room to check on her, but she was half-asleep.

"Sarah?" I asked, kneeling down beside the couch.

Her eyes fluttered open, still red and puffy from crying, "Yes?"

"Would it be okay if I stay here with you tonight?"

Tears started to well up in her eyes again, and she nodded. I kissed her forehead, brushing my lips carefully against her soft skin. I had never wanted to care for someone so much.

"I've got to go get a few things from the B&B, but I'll be back in a little while, okay?"

She nodded again, then wiped her tears on her sleeve and rolled over. As I walked away, I heard her sniffle and mumble something that sounded like, "Thanks for being here for me, Emily."

It was late enough in the afternoon that the sun was almost set, and the cold winter wind howled through the streets blowing leftover snow, and scattering it over the sidewalks. It was so cold, the blistering wind soaked through my jacket before I made it back to the B&B.

I could hear pots and pans clanging in the kitchen when I went in. I walked up the stairs to my room, and packed a bag with a couple of my outfits and some toiletries, leaving about half my stuff still in my drawers. On my way down the stairs, I saw John emerge from the kitchen.

"Hey, Emily. We are just making some dinner. Did you want some?"

"No, that's okay. I'm not hungry."

"Is everything okay?" he asked.

"Yeah, it's just been a long day."

"So, are you running away, then?"

"Oh, this?" I looked down at the small suitcase I had beside me, "No, I'm just going to spend a little extra time with Sarah right now."

"That sounds nice," he smiled, turning to go back into the kitchen. Before he finished crossing the dining room, he turned back around to face me, "Emily?"

"Yes?"

"What do you think of Kiuchi?"

"What do I think of her? She's nice. Why?"

"I was going to invite her out here for a visit. What do you think?"

"I think," I started, pausing to think about what had just happened at Sarah's house, "I think you should talk to her parents."

John laughed out loud, "Her parents? She is a grown adult, and so am I."

"So? She might care what her parents think. She might want her parents to approve of her and to be okay with her choices. She might want her parents in her life, and if you do something that upsets her parents, you will hurt her. Maybe they won't want you guys together."

John looked at me with a raised eyebrow, "Wow, okay then. Merry Christmas to you."

John disappeared into the kitchen, and I slipped out the front door with my bag.

The weight of my heart slowed my footsteps as I wandered the streets in the bitter cold. I couldn't convince myself to go back to Sarah's house yet. I had one more place I needed to stop. One more 'Merry Christmas' to say.

Chapter 26

My parents' gravestones were covered in a thin layer of ice. I knelt down in front of them, tears streaming down my face. I hated them, and yet, I was devastated that I was unable to share that Christmas with them. I couldn't tell them what had happened to me.

"You would hate me, if you saw me now," I laughed, wiping tears from my stinging cheeks, "I'm not just the kid that ran away to California. Now, I'm going to be divorced, and I'm dating another woman. Her name is Sarah, and her parents found out about us today.

"She lost them. They are alive, but they want nothing to do with her now, and I can't help thinking it's because of me. Today is Christmas, and it always reminds me of how I lost you. And now I caused Sarah to lose her parents, too. Everything is falling apart. I just wish I knew what you would say right now. I wish you were here."

My tears fell to the ground, turning into ice on top of the layer of snow that I was kneeling in. The church bells chimed, low and mournful in the tower above me, and groups of people poured out of the church, clutching their coats to them as the wind howled.

Light streamed out from behind the large wooden doors, and my feet were suddenly under me, walking me towards the warmth of the church, with my bag dragging through the snow behind me. The moment I stepped inside, I was hit with a wave of heat, and my hands began to tingle as the feeling returned to them. I left my suitcase in a corner by the front door.

There were a few people still left in the pews, praying in silence, but for the most part, the church was empty. It was exactly as I remembered it from when I was a little girl: hollow and intimidating. The ceiling was a few stories up, with curved wood holding up the roof. The walls were cream, and the pews were dark wood, with red cushions on the seats and kneelers.

The altar, tabernacle, and candle holders were all shiny gold. And the central decoration in the church was a large crucifix of Jesus on the cross, covered in blood, which hung on the wall above the altar. It was roughly the size of a bus.

To the right of the pews was a small wooden door to a back room. Above the door was a sign that read 'Confession' and another sign beside it which read 'Open.'

My feet, which had led my numb body into the church for warmth, led me over to the confession door, seeking answers. I entered the little room and took a seat, just as I had done a hundred time as a child.

"Tell me your sins, my child," the priest said in a heavy tone through a black mesh screen. I didn't recognize his voice as any priest I knew, so I felt calm enough to open up a bit about what I was going through.

138

"Well, you see, I have been getting ready to divorce my husband," I said, looking down at the floor and fidgeting with my coat.

"You know that divorce is a sin?"

"Yes," I answered, not really believing it.

It was then that I knew how Sarah was so easily able to forget that she was an adult and become submissive to her parents. I could feel myself reverting back to the same thoughts and feelings of guilt that I had years before.

"Then why do you seek to divorce your husband?"

"I'm afraid of him. I don't want to be hit anymore."

"I see. Well, I'm sure that with repentance and prayer, the Lord shall forgive you, so long as you do not seek another until it is annulled. Are there any other sins you wish to confess?"

I rubbed my hands together, trying to get rid of my nerves, "Yes, I need advice. I think I already know what you are going to say, but the obvious answers don't feel right."

"Don't make assumptions, child," he assured, "God is mysterious."

"Well, there is this woman. I want to be with her in a way that I have never wanted to be with another woman before."

"Homosexuality is a sin. You know this?"

"Yes. The whole idea is very new to me, and yet it feels natural to be with her. I don't know what to do," I sighed, covering my face with my hands.

"Well, do you love her?" asked the priest.

"Do I love her?" I repeated his question, searching my thoughts for an answer, "Wait, does that even matter?"

I heard the priest sigh, and there was a pause before he answered, "The Bible teaches us that love covers over sins, that there is no power greater than love, and that God is love. Of course, the Catholic Church is not accepting of homosexuality, and I am not saying that it is not a sin. It is. But what I am saying is that love, itself, is of God."

"Do I love her?" I repeated again, this time in a whisper.

"Let me ask it in this way," he said, "When you do things for her or spend time with her, do you do it for selfish reasons, or do you do it for her and her happiness?"

I thought back over my experiences with her. There were definitely a lot of things that I had done, that to me, felt selfish. But after everything that had happened with her family, all I wanted was to see her happy again. If that meant being with her more often, I would. And if that meant leaving her alone, I would do that, too. I just wanted her to be okay.

"I love her," I answered, a bit shocked at the way the words seemed to flow so easily out of my mouth.

"There is your answer," he said, "Pray your rosary ten times and ask for forgiveness. Peace be with you, child."

"I love her!" I said, much louder this time.

I leaped from my seat, throwing open the door to the confessional. I snatched my bag up from beside the front doors to the church, and I dashed down the street back to Sarah's house.

Chapter 27

I burst through the front door of Sarah's house and threw off my coat and hat. I left the suitcase by the door and flew to the living room, dropping down beside her. She was awake, lying down on the couch and playing some sort of shooting game on the TV.

"Sarah! I'm back, and I brought enough stuff to stay for days if you'd like," I said, grinning and looking over her expression.

She paused her game and looked down at me with wide eyes, "Really?"

"Yes, really. I want to spend time with you. I want to be here with you."

She put her controller aside and jumped up throwing pulling me up from the ground and hugging me, jumping up and down, "Yay! I'm so excited! Thank you, Emily."

I stepped back, my face hurting from how much I was smiling. "And it's still Christmas. There is a lot of food made that I packed up and put in the fridge. Should we warm it up and have some dinner?"

"That sounds nice," she smiled, "Do you play video games?"

"No, not really. I've never really tried it," I shrugged.

"Could I maybe show you after dinner? It always helps me destress, and I never get to play with other people unless I play online. I'd love to play with you."

"Sure, that sounds like fun."

Sarah and I warmed up some sugared yams, the stir-fried vegetables, and finished cooking the roast duck. The food had a bit of a leftover taste, even though it was only made earlier that day, but it was still filling.

"Emily?" Sarah asked, pushing the vegetables around on her plate with her fork, "Do you think my parents will ever talk to me again?"

"I don't know," I said, folding my hands on my lap and looking down at my own plate, "But the important thing is that you have time to find out."

"What do you mean?"

"Well," I sighed, "Earlier today, I went to talk to my parents about us."

"Are they still around here?" she asked, looking excited for a moment.

"They are buried at the graveyard by the Catholic church."

"Oh…I'm so sorry."

"It's okay. Honestly, I really never liked my parents, and I don't think they would like me very much now, either. But there is part of me that I wish I could know for sure. I want to be able to tell them about my life and who I've become. And about…" I trailed off, thinking over whether I should tell her about my revelation from confession.

She was looking at me quietly with teary eyes.

143

"Never mind," I said, shaking my head, "So, what kind of video games are you going to teach me about?"

Her eyes lit up a little bit, and she snatched up our plates and set them down in the kitchen before coming back out and pulling out a black zipper case from beside the TV.

"No, no, no," she mumbled, flipping through the discs before stopping at one, "Yes! Let's try *World War Space*. We each pick a country and two other countries to back us up, and then we fight in space on different planets and stuff with laser guns. It's really fun."

I laughed. Her enthusiasm illuminated her face, and she practically bounced up and down. She was so adorable I just wanted to kiss her.

"Okay, that sounds like an interesting game."

We sat down on the couch together, and she went over all the buttons with me. I probably died something like 100 times before I ever actually shot anyone, but after about an hour, I started to get the hang of it, and we had a lot of fun. We laughed and shot laser guns and blew things up in an imaginary world. And for a little while, the real world became a little easier to handle.

I wasn't sure how long we played the game for, but eventually we ended up cuddling on the couch, holding hands, fast asleep. It was a cozy Christmas night.

I stayed at her house until New Year's Eve when we went back to the B&B for a little party. John was well enough to work again, and he had helped

Margaret check out the visiting families the day before, so it was just us four.

Most of the Christmas decorations were still up, but John had set up his phone on the mantle with a live video of the ball drop in Times Square. Margaret passed out shiny silver party hats and pink champagne. Her demeanor made it appear she might have already had a few glasses.

Sarah wore the locket I had given her, and she held my hand openly during the party. I finally felt like we were turning into a real couple. John spent some time video-chatting with Kiuchi, and it was nice to see him so happy and excited. His face was almost completely healed.

While we were all together, I decided to turn in my job application to Margaret. I wasn't sure how much time Sarah would have to spend together once school started up again after the holidays, so I just marked that I was always available, and I was going to let Margaret decide my schedule for me.

As the time got closer to midnight, we all sat together on the couches with our drinks in our hands, watching the small screen of John's phone anxiously.

10…9…8…7…6…5…knock, knock, knock. There was someone at the door. I was closest to it, so I let go of Sarah's hand to go and answer it. 4…3…2…I opened the door, and the cold air from the street rushed in. 1…there was celebratory cheering from the living room, but I couldn't make a sound. I stood, frozen in place, staring into the eyes of the man in the doorway. It was Hector.

Chapter 28

"I come in peace," he smirked, holding his hands up. "I just wanted to talk to you."

I felt like running, throwing up, or both. But I didn't do anything. I just stood there, watching him. He was dressed in an expensive-looking gray wool coat and thrown over one of his black business suits. His hair was trimmed perfectly, and he was clean-shaven. He didn't look angry, or sad, or anything. He wore his usual confident demeanor.

"Listen," he said, putting his hands in his pockets, "I get the message. We are over. But that means we have some official paperwork to take care of. I brought the divorce documents, and I thought we might go over them and get them signed tomorrow night over dinner. I'll fax them right over to the lawyers, and that will be that. You can be done with me."

I was stunned. He had never been this reasonable in the past. It was always about his way and getting what he wanted out of me. And he shouldn't have even been there. I'd filled out that restraining order. Just being on the front porch was a violation of it. His look made me suspicious, but I did want to get a divorce.

146

"Fine," I said, "But we have to meet someplace public."

"Zach's Steakhouse, 6:00?"

I nodded, starting to close the door.

His hand reached out and stopped it with a bang, "And let's keep this between you and me, okay, sugar? Happy New Year, Emily."

His hand slid off the door and he straightened out his coat and turned around, walking down the street to a limo that was waiting for him. I slammed the door and double locked it.

I then went back into the living room to join everyone again. My mind was blank. I felt like a zombie, drained of all my energy. I picked up my cold glass of champagne and downed the whole thing in one big gulp.

"Who was at the door?" Margaret asked.

"No one," I said stiffly.

She raised an eyebrow at me, "Okay. Well, John was just getting ready to tell us some exciting news. John?"

"Kiuchi is going to come and visit from next week until Valentine's Day. She will be staying with her family in the area, but we will get to go on real dates together."

"That's wonderful, darling," said Margaret, clapping her hands together.

"And, Sarah and Emily, I want you guys to go on a double date with us," he added.

"Yeah, okay. That sounds fun," I said, staring off at the wall. *How did he find me? Was I in danger?*

"I agree," she said, "It would be nice to go on an actual date in public together."

I wanted to smile, but I was still numb from the shock of seeing Hector. So, instead, I asked, "Is there any more champagne?"

I had two more glasses before the party ended. When Sarah got all bundled up to leave, I was too terrified to follow her outside.

"I think I'm going to stay here tonight," I explained, "I start work here tomorrow, and so I think it would be best to sleep here. Plus, I had a lot to drink, and I kind of just want to go lay down."

"Oh, alright. Well, don't hide away from me for too long," she smiled, leaving a kiss on my cheek.

As soon as she left, I crawled up the stairs, and down the hall to the pink room. I laid on top of the covers, and stared at the ceiling all night. My mind just flashed images across my eyes of my past with Hector, and it kept replaying what had just happened at the door. I felt like I was in some sort of waking nightmare. Somehow, he had found me.

The next day went really fast. Margaret had me going through paperwork and finalizing payment information for a group of guys who would be our guests the following week for some sort of 21st-birthday event. Once I had finished all the paperwork for each of the guests and filed it all away, it was already 5 o'clock.

To get ready for dinner, I put on a cream turtleneck and a pair of jeans, and I brushed my hair out. I didn't put on makeup, perfume, or anything that might have made him think that I was trying to win him back. *This is going to be easy…*I told myself…*Just go and sign the papers, and you will never have to see him again.*

I really wanted to tell Margaret where I was going when she asked. I hated hiding stuff from her, especially after all she had done for me. But I didn't want to make her worry any more than she needed to. It was just a dinner.

I took an Uber to the restaurant and walked in with as much confidence as I could muster. The restaurant was decorated with casual wood benches with laminated menus and animal heads of all different kinds hanging on the walls. Hector was sitting in the back corner, drinking some sort of alcohol, and there was an empty place already set across from him. With shaky legs, I crossed the restaurant and took my seat.

Chapter 29

"Ah, Emily, so glad you made it," he said, picking up his menu and looking over it, "You know, I never go to such cheap restaurants, but I thought this would be the ideal place for us to meet. I like steak, and apparently, you want to live out in the country with a bunch of nobody's."

And there he was, the condescending man that was, at least for a little while longer, my husband.

"Did you bring the paperwork?" I asked, sipping my water.

"I did," he said, putting down his menu, "But there are a few things I want to go over before we sign."

"Are you guys ready to order?" asked the waiter. He definitely looked more like a greasy bodybuilder than a waiter, though.

"Yes," answered Hector, "I will have an 8oz T-bone steak. Rare. With mashed potatoes. And she will have the garden salad with the fat-free Italian dressing."

"Got it. Should be out in just a few minutes," the waiter said, taking our menus.

I sighed, irritated that he would order that for me. "Why couldn't you just let me order my own food? Maybe I wanted steak, too."

"You are still my wife. You gotta keep that figure slim for me," he winked.

"Not for long," I hissed.

"Speaking of that," he said, taking a casual sip of his drink with one hand. His other hand was hidden in his lap. And then, I heard the click of a gun cock from under our table.

He leaned towards me, "Let's get something straight. The only reason I am going to divorce you is because I don't want to be married to a pathetic bitch like you. You embarrassed me, and you don't appreciate anything I've ever given you.

"If I find out that you are doing this to leave me for someone else, I swear to God, I will kill you both. If you go to the police, you are dead. Do you really think some piece of paper could keep me away from you? You obviously have no idea who I am."

It was impossible to breathe, and I had to squeeze my hands together until there was almost no blood left in them to keep them from shaking. I started to get dizzy like I was going to pass out, so I took a few deep breaths to try and calm down, but even those were painful.

I heard another click and the moving of cloth, as he put the gun away and brought both hands back into view, placing a briefcase on the table and opening it. He pulled out a stack of papers and passed them to me.

"Basically, it says I get everything, and you get nothing. You can look it over if you want, but if you want to change anything, you will need to get a lawyer of your own," he explained, passing me a pen.

151

He was right. It basically stated that he was going to have possession of the house, the cars, the investment funds, all the furniture, and all the money, with the exception of any money I had in cash or any personal accounts that I had. There were yellow tabs where I was supposed to sign, and with trembling hands, I did.

"Good," he said, "And now that we have everything cleared up, we can eat," he said, taking the paperwork and putting it away again.

The waiter dropped off our food a few minutes later, and Hector scarfed his down. I barely touched mine. I wasn't hungry, and I felt like I'd swallowed a knife.

"So that's it?" I asked, "Are we divorced?"

"Well, I have to fax these over tonight. They should have them turned in sometime next week, and then there is a 30 day waiting period for it to be finalized. You will receive a confirmation letter in the mail."

"Okay," I answered. But I was definitely not okay. I had to be married to Hector for another month.

"And speaking of 30 days," he said, wiping the blood from his steak off his mouth with a paper napkin, "I'll be staying here in town just to be sure that everything goes smoothly."

"What about work?" I asked, trying to sound casual about it.

"I've made arrangements for while I'm away. I won't be needing to leave any time soon."

I nodded slowly, taking another small bite of salad and trying to process my new situation. *What was I going to tell Sarah?*

"Here is the check whenever you are ready," said the waiter, dropping off a paper receipt at the edge of our table.

"I'll get it," said Hector, snatching it up, "You are probably running pretty low on funds by now." He opened his wallet and threw down far too much cash, then slipped on his gray coat. "Tik, Tok."

In just a few long strides, he was out of the restaurant. My stomach churned, and I ran to the bathroom, heaving up everything I had eaten and gasping for air.

One month. I had to survive for one month under the watchful guard of Hector Jacobson. A man with wealth, power, and a gun.

Chapter 30

I had to break up with Sarah. At least, that was the only option I could think of. I had to protect her from him. I wanted so badly to go to the cops, but for all I knew, he had paid them off or something. I felt so helpless.

I knocked on Sarah's door, and she answered in her pajamas.

"Hi, Emily," she yawned, "You here to stay the night again?"

"No. I need to get my things."

"You look sick. Is everything okay?"

"No," I answered, tears stinging my eyes, "I can't see you anymore. Not for the next month."

"Like, you will be too busy? Or you don't want to see me?"

"I want to, I just…I can't explain it right now. I can't tell you any more than that. I can't be with you."

"Okay, I'm sorry," she said, stepping aside, "You can go get your things."

I rushed by her and gathered up all of my clothes, my toothbrush, and everything that was mine as quickly as I could. I stuffed it all into my suitcase and walked back out the front door.

"Emily?" Sarah called after me. Her voice cracked, "Can we still be friends?"

I wanted to keep Sarah out of his line of sight completely. But on the other hand, I knew I couldn't just leave her like that. Leaving her wasn't my choice, it was just something I had to do.

"Yes, I suppose so," I answered, not turning around, "We can't spend a lot of time together, though. Not right now. But, I promise, I'll explain it all next month. I'm sorry."

There was a heavy silence for just a moment, and then I heard her door click shut, and my heart shattered into a million little pieces as I walked away, back to the B&B.

The next couple of weeks passed in a blur. John was out with Kiuchi a lot of the time, so I picked up the slack at the B&B. We had a few people coming in and out to stay in the area for various events and family occasions. I kept as busy as I could, but I couldn't seem to stop thinking about Sarah. I refused to leave the B&B, though. I didn't want to run into Hector.

One night, when John came home from a date with Kiuchi, he stopped in the kitchen where I was doing the dishes, and he took my hand. He looked at me with piercing eyes.

"Emily, I need to talk to you."

I turned off the water and dried my hands on a towel, "Sure, whatsup?"

"You haven't gone to see Sarah at all since New Year's, and this morning, I saw her in town, and she looked really depressed. What happened?"

"We are taking a little break for a few weeks while I get myself together," I shrugged, turning back to the dishes.

"Emily," he urged, catching my arm with his hand, "She trusts you. I trust you. Please, what's going on? You've been acting funny for over two weeks."

"I can tell you after Valentine's Day," I said plainly.

"Fine," he huffed, "Does this mean no double date?"

My heart sank at the idea. I really wanted to see Sarah again, and if we were in a group, maybe it wouldn't look like a date. But I didn't want to put her in danger. "I can go with Sarah as friends."

"Well, then, it really isn't a double date, is it?"

"I just…I can't be seen with her in public. Not right now."

"Well, then, why don't we have it here? Would you be okay with seeing her here?" he asked, practically begging.

"I don't know. I guess? I'd like the chance to talk with her," I shrugged, looking down at the floor.

"Great! Let's do it this Friday night. I have so much to tell you guys, but I want us all together," he smiled, patting me on the back and leaving the kitchen.

I finished up the dishes and went up to my room to destress a bit. I still hadn't started creating a piece for the art show yet, but I still had some supplies tucked away from when I had been taking Sarah's class.

I pulled out my sketchbook and flipped it to a clean white sheet of paper. My pencil was a little dull, but I'd forgotten to get a sharpener, so I just tried to start the outline of something.

At first, I started to try and draw some sort of flower bouquet, but all it made me want to do was give flowers to Sarah. And so, I erased it and tried to draw a picture of a beach, but all I could think of was Sarah and I at the beach together.

I tore the paper to shreds, and put my pencil and sketchpad away. Sarah helped inspire me to do art again, so I decided that I wanted to do a portrait of Sarah, my Valentine, for the Valentine's Art Show. But I was going to need her to model for it.

Chapter 31

That Friday, I was a ball of nerves. I had seen Hector stalking me at the grocery store the day before when Margaret had sent me to pick up some ingredients for her recipes. I'd been avoiding going out for her, but I knew she needed help, so it was hard to turn her down. Hector didn't directly look at me in the store. He simply walked down every aisle I was in, pretending to look at items, and disappeared when I went to the checkout counter. He was watching me, and it made me paranoid.

A part of me wanted to cancel the night with everyone. I knew that I was putting them in danger, even if it was just a dinner at the B&B. But I really wanted to see Sarah again. Even if I couldn't touch her, I could still be near her.

I put on a little black dress and did my makeup like it was a date, including red lipstick. I even put waves in my hair with some of John's gel that he let me borrow. John and Kiuchi were also dressed up. But I felt a little foolish when Sarah arrived.

"Oh, I didn't know it was a formal event. I thought we were just friends hanging out and having dinner," she explained, her cheeks blushing. She was dressed in one of her hoodies and a pair of jeans. "Maybe I should go home."

"No, you look beautiful," I said, "You know what? Let me go and change. I'll be right back."

I darted upstairs and wiped off my makeup and threw on my skinny jeans and a pink long-sleeve t-shirt. I grabbed my sketchpad and pencil on my way back downstairs so I could ask her about doing a portrait.

John had been cooking most of the afternoon. He had made all of us a spaghetti dinner with garlic bread and salad, and it looked like it came from a fine restaurant. Sarah sat awkwardly beside me at dinner, and she didn't look at me once. John and Kiuchi, on the other hand, were living in their own little world, spending the first half of the meal giggling and whispering back and forth to each other.

Eventually, John looked up at me, and his smile faded. He took a sip of his wine and tried to start a conversation. "So, um, Emily, do you have anything cool planned in the next few weeks?"

"Actually," I said, turning to Sarah, "I need to make my art piece for the Valentine's show. I was wondering if maybe you would model for me, Sarah?"

"Model? I'm not much of a model," she shrugged, taking another bite of her garlic bread.

"I really wanted to make a piece that represented Valentine's Day. I thought of you," I explained.

"Yeah, I guess friends are kind of a part of Valentine's Day. At least, that's what I teach my students. Sure, I'll model for you. When do you want to hang out?"

159

"I've got my stuff right here," I said, pulling out my sketchpad and pencil from beside me, "I was hoping to get the base sketch done tonight."

"Um, okay. How do you want me?"

"Just the way you are," I smiled, taking the pencil and starting to shape her face on the page.

She smiled, too, took a sip of red wine, and then turned to face me, running her hands through her curls.

"Glad to see you two hanging out again," said John.

"Me too," I said, trying not to blush while I was sketching Sarah's bright eyes. "So, Kiuchi, how are you enjoying your visit?"

"Very good," she answered with a little giggle, "John is so nice."

Kiuchi was short and petite with long dark hair. Her eyes were deep and dark, and she always had a bouncy energy about her, even though she came across as a bit shy. She was always dressed in bright floral blouses with slacks and heels, and I wondered what she did for work that always had her dressed so nicely.

"Kiuchi and I actually have some news that we wanted to share with you guys. It's kind of why we wanted this dinner," said John, straightening himself up and giving Kiuchi a wink, "You want to tell them, honey?"

"We are engaged!" Kiuchi squealed, showing us her hand, which now held a small diamond on a gold band.

"Oh, wow! Congratulations. That is so wonderful," I exclaimed, and I stood to get up and hug them both.

"Thank you," they said together in unison.

"So happy for you," said Sarah, smiling from her seat.

As I made my way back to my chair, eager to hear more about their engagement, I was suddenly hit with a wave of anxiety. In the corner of my eye, I spotted a man, standing in the window of the dining room, looking in. I did a double-take. He was definitely there. We locked eyes, and with a wink, Hector slumped back away from the window and into the shadows.

"Thanks for the dinner, it was fun. I've really got to get to bed, though. I'm tired. Goodnight, everyone. Congrats, John," I said, my words all running together.

"What about the portrait?" Sarah called after me.

"I've got enough done. Thanks," I yelled back in a shaky voice.

I scooped up my sketchbook and pencil and sprinted up the stairs, taking two steps at a time, in the same way, that you run out of a room when you are afraid of the dark.

Once I was up in my room, I tossed my art supplies under the bed, closed the curtains tightly, making sure that there were no cracks that could be seen through. Then I locked the door, turned out the lights, jumped into bed, pulled the covers over my head, and cried myself to sleep.

Chapter 32

I barely slept or ate for the next two weeks. I did my work for Margaret, but I avoided the windows everywhere I went. Margaret assumed I had some sort of cold. She always pointed out that I was pale and that my nose was red from using tissues. I simply agreed with her and would go back to my chores. It was a good cover because she wouldn't send me out of the house for errands and often encouraged me to drink tea and take naps, which kept me up in my room most of the time.

I had finished the sketch layer for Sarah's portrait, but it needed color. Bright, vibrant color. I wanted it to not only look like her, but also feel like her. When people saw it, I wanted them to love her.

"Hey, Margaret?" I asked, peeking around the corner of the kitchen.

She was whipping up a batch of cookies. "Yes?"

"Do we have any bright paints or other art supplies in the storage room? I have a few supplies, but I would like to use something different, if possible."

"We should have something artsy down there," she answered, plopping cookie dough onto a baking sheet, "Are you sure you are going to be okay, Emily? I can take you to the hospital if you need. You have been sick for a long time."

"I'll be okay," I sighed, "Hopefully, this will all be better in only a few more days."

"Okay, sweetie."

I went down into the basement through a small door under the stairs. It was where John and Margaret kept all the decorations and extra supplies for the B&B. I rummaged through boxes of holiday decorations, crates of tools, clear bins filled with extra pillows and blankets, and a couple boxes that were filled with unidentifiable pieces of broken objects.

Then, I came to a box with office supplies in it, which was closer to what I had been looking for. Inside were printer paper, pens, boxes of staples, and highlighters. I shoved my hand down a little deeper into the box, just to be sure there wasn't anything else, and my hand came in contact with a box about the size of a thick book. I pulled it up through the rest of the supplies, and a spark of creativity rushed through me when I saw what it was.

It was a box of 100 crayons. Sarah, the woman who I wanted to show to the world, who was a bright light in my darkness, just so happened to be a kindergarten teacher. It was brilliant. I was going to paint her with crayons. The colors were bright, just like her, and the medium represented who she was and what she loved. I packed the box back up and put it away, happily taking my box of crayons upstairs.

"Oh, Emily," Margaret said, coming into the foyer and wiping her hands on her new daisy apron, "I almost forgot to tell you that some mail came for you yesterday. It's sitting on the coffee table."

My heart began to feel a little lighter, "Mail?" I strode into the living room and laid the box of crayons on the couch beside me. There, on the coffee table, was a yellow envelope from the county courts in California. I picked it up, squeezing the prongs and carefully ripping it open. I pulled out the pack of papers and read the cover page.

It was a letter officially announcing that the divorce had been finalized. Behind it was a copy of the divorce decree and all the paperwork we had signed. It was official: I was free.

My tears fell onto the papers, causing wet circles to soak into the pages, and the ink bled where they fell. I hugged them tightly to my body, rocking back and forth. I felt relieved, I felt hope, and yet, there was also a twinge of guilt. But it was easily melted away by my realization that I was free to see Sarah. I was no longer under Hector's thumb. He was gone.

I ran to Margaret and cried happily on her shoulder, "I'm divorced. It's official."

"Thank God, Emily! I'm so happy for you. But I'm sorry, I know it must be hard at the same time. Are you okay? Is there anything I can get you?"

"Thank you so much, Margaret. For everything. Really. You and John have saved my life. I'm going to be okay. But now I have to go upstairs and finish my artwork for the show. It's in two days."

"Are you going to talk to Sarah?" she asked.

"This portrait will say it all, I think," I answered.

I went back to the living room to get my crayons and paperwork, then I took them all upstairs to get my work done. I had a plan, and it needed to be ready by Valentine's Day.

Chapter 33

The art show was at six, but Sarah had told me to bring the art to the library at four so that she could make sure everything was set up for the reception. Because I walked instead of getting a ride, I thought I might be a few minutes late, but I was light on my feet, and I got there just in time.

I entered the library, which was small and quiet, with only about 50 large bookshelves or so lined up around the middle of the floor. There were couches and reading tables, all brown and tattered, scattered here and there. And there was a young, grumpy-looking librarian at the desk, typing some things into a computer. Her clothes were bright pink, but her energy was dark, and she obviously wasn't pleased with whatever she was working on.

"Hello, miss?" I asked, "I am looking for Sarah Norman? I'm supposed to drop off some art for the show."

"Ah, yes. Back room," she pointed to a glass door to her left without looking up from the computer, "She is back there right now. That's where the show will be tonight."

"Thank you."

I put my hand on the cold metal handle, took a breath, and opened the door. Sarah was there, hanging up a large metal-framed painting on the back wall. She was dressed in a friendly yellow sweater over some khakis with a pair of sneakers. Her hair was tied up in a loose bun, which had a few pencils sticking out of it.

"Sarah?" I asked hesitantly.

"Oh, hi, Emily," her voice wasn't excited or energetic like it usually was. She sounded tired, "I'll be with you in a moment."

She centered the painting, which was some kind of modern art drip painting in black and white, and then she turned around and came to stand in front of me with her arms crossed.

"Sarah," I started, holding my piece of paper to myself so she couldn't see yet.

"That has to be in a frame," she sighed.

"Ah, well, I will go do that. But first, I need to talk to you."

"Okay, just make it quick. I have a lot to do before the reception," she said, wiping a tear from her cheek.

"Sarah," I started again, "I know that I left abruptly and I probably hurt you. But I was trying to protect you. My ex-husband found me here and wanted to fill out divorce papers. I did. But he stayed in town until they went through, and he stalked me.

"I was afraid to go to the police, and he threatened to kill me or anyone I was close to if he thought I might be romantically involved with anyone. The divorce is final, so I can be with you now. I just couldn't tell you all this before. I wanted to protect you because I…I love…"

"I love you, too," interrupted Sarah, wrapping me in her arms and holding me tightly with a sigh.

"Wait, you aren't mad? I thought you were mad at me."

"No," she cried, "I just wanted to give you the space you wanted. I've been wanting you to come back every day. But I didn't want to scare you off. I could tell something was wrong. And I used the time away to think, as well. I missed you so much. I'd rather show you off to the world and be judged for it than go another day without you by my side. I'm okay with being public about our relationship if that's what you want."

I hugged her tighter. I couldn't seem to get close enough to her. I was overwhelmed with joy, excitement, and love. The picture made a crinkling sound in my hand.

"Oh, yeah," I said, stepping back and turning the picture around to show her, "Will you be my Valentine?"

I had drawn her smiling in the glowing way she did when I first met her at the Halloween party. Her hair was down, and the background was angel wings shaped like the ones on her tree. On her chest was a heart, drawn simply like her students might draw a heart, made with bright red crayon.

Her hands covered her mouth, and her eyes were wide, "It's so beautiful, Emily. Thank you."

She took it from me to examine it closer, and her face lit up in a smile.

"I'm so glad you like it."

"And yes!" she exclaimed, "Yes, I will be your Valentine." She reached down into her sweater and pulled out the locket.

"I don't know what to say. I didn't know if you were going to want me back. I just…" I stuttered.

"I'm so glad you finally got your divorce and that you are okay. That's so scary that he came here. Is he gone?" she asked, looking over my shoulder.

"Yeah, I think so. I didn't see him on my walk over here, and recently, if I went out at all, I would run into him."

"Well, good," she smiled, "I have a frame I can put this in for the show. I have a lot to get done here right now, but maybe we can do something after. See you at the show at six?"

"Absolutely," I answered.

I kissed her on her cheek, and I left the library with a skip in my step to go back to the B&B and get ready for the night.

Chapter 34

Margaret drove, and John and Kiuchi sat in the back seat. They had decided to come to the show before their Valentine's dinner date. I sat in the front with Margaret and spent most of the ride looking out the window for any sign of Hector. I didn't see anything that indicated he was there, and I settled back into my seat.

There were actually quite a few cars in the parking lot, and some people had even started parking on the street. I smoothed down my skirt as I stepped out of the car, wondering to myself if maybe I had overdone my outfit. I'd dressed in a red dress and leggings with my heels and my red jacket to celebrate the holiday. I was feeling festive, knowing that Sarah would be waiting there for me.

We all went into the back room of the library, and it had really been spruced up since I had seen it a few hours before. There were red streamers hanging from the ceiling, a snack and drink table by the door with cans of soda and bags of chips and cookies, and about 20 or so different paintings in all different styles hanging around the walls of the room.

"Let's go find your piece," said Margaret, taking my arm and joining the line of people who were slowly making their way around the room.

My drawing was on the back wall next to the modern piece I had seen Sarah hanging earlier and a landscape painting of what looked like the local town hall building. A part of me felt like snatching my drawing down off the wall so no one else could see it.

There were some amazing artists displaying their work there. Some of the paintings looked so realistic they could have been photographs. And then, there was my piece, all colored with crayons. At least I knew that Sarah liked it. When we finished making our way around the room of abstract paintings and artistic portraits, we stopped to grab a few sodas at the snack table.

"Hello, everyone. Can I have your attention?" came Sarah's voice over a set of speakers. She was standing up in the front of the room by my drawing, holding a microphone. "I wanted to thank you all for coming to this year's Valentine's Art Show. I'd like to take a moment to put a spotlight on our debut artists and to make a few announcements."

Sarah's hair was put up with a sparkling black hair clip, and she was wearing a tight black cocktail dress with a big red sequenced heart-shaped pin on her left shoulder. On her legs she wore black tights and black boots that went up to her knees. She looked hot, and I felt better about my dress, as well.

"Our first artist is Lin Zhu, and this is her painting right here. She is a local color-blind artist. She uses her life in black and white as inspiration to paint

171

the beauty of these contrasting colors for others to enjoy."

The whole room clapped, and Lin Zhu stepped forward to stand beside Sarah and give a bow, before returning to the crowd. She was a young Asian woman in her 30s, and she was dressed in a very artistic black and white cocktail dress with huge black hoop earrings that touched her shoulders under her waist-length hair.

"I guess you should probably get closer to the front so you can go bow when she announces your art," whispered John.

I nodded and took a step forward to start pushing my way through the crowd. But I was stopped by a hand on my shoulder. I turned to see who it was that was grabbing me so tightly, and I thought I might faint when I did. Hector had a hold of me, and his face was smug as he took off his sunglasses with his other hand.

"You didn't think I'd leave without a goodbye, did you?" he asked with a wink.

"I'm calling the police," whispered Margaret in my ear before sneaking away behind me.

"The second debut artist we have tonight," Sarah continued, "Is Nicholas Lowery. He is a traveling artist who paints beautiful landmarks from the different towns he visits. This is his painting of the Maple Creek Town Hall. We are so excited to have you here, Mr. Lowery." The room applauded again, and I knew my turn was next.

"Let me go, Hector," I growled, shoving his arm off of me.

"What's going on?" asked John, turning from his conversation with Kiuchi to look at me.

"And our final guest is someone very close to my heart," announced Sarah into the loud speakers.

I stepped forward again, pushing through the crowd to the front of the room. I could feel Hector close behind me.

"Emily Heart drew this portrait of me as a Valentine's gift. She is a special woman who has made my life a little brighter and my holidays a little cheaper. I don't know what I'd do without you. Happy Valentine's Day, Emily."

This time, there was less applause and more hushed whispers as people conversed between themselves about what she had just said. I was pushed by the last person in front of the crowd, stood beside Sarah, and took a bow. She reached down and took my hand, and I tried to snatch it away before Hector saw. I wanted to warn Sarah, but it was too late.

"Wait, what?" I heard Hector's booming voice, "You did leave me for someone else? And it's a woman? You pathetic little cunt!"

He raised a strong hand in the air, but before it could swing down on me, someone caught it from behind him. It was John. Within seconds, John's fist smashed across the side of Hector's jaw, and he fell to the floor with a thud.

The door to the art showroom swung open, and two police officers stepped in, "We are looking for a Hector Jacobson?"

The room parted a path for the officers that led straight up to Hector, who was still struggling to get up from the floor. After taking a few statements from John, Margaret, and me, Hector was taken away in the police car. Then we went back into the art show like nothing had happened.

Sarah threw her arms around me, "Oh, my goodness, that was terrifying," she said.

The scent of her vanilla perfume and her body pressed against mine sent a tingling shock through me.

"I think it's over," I said, relief washing over me, "And are you okay? You know, now that we are public?"

"Yeah, I will be. Some people in there are angry, but my boss, the principal, actually came over to talk to me. He said that his son was gay, and he thought it was brave of me to speak out after all this time. So, I guess I get to keep my job," she shrugged.

"I'm so glad," I said with a sigh.

"So," she said, pulling away, "What do you say we get out of here and have a real Valentine's Day?"

"I'd like that," I smiled.

I took one last look back at the room. John and Kiuchi happily conversed in the corner over cans of cola, and Margaret talked with some artists about their paintings of a kitten. Everything was finally okay. And I no longer wondered where I belonged or where I was going to go. I was home in Maple Creek.

Sarah and I left the art show, hand in hand, as we made our way back to her place for a Valentine's evening full of pizza, video games, and most of all, love.

About the Author

Elizabeth Penn has spent her life travelling the world, and was inspired by the diversity of her friends and family to write books that could represent the complexities of love in all its forms. Elizabeth studied Creative Writing and English at SNHU. The only thing she loves more than writing is being a mom.

For more from her, go to:
pennromance.com